Baron Bc

D0969278

ALSO BY ALEXANDER LERNET-HOLENIA

Count Luna

ALEXANDER
LERNET-HOLENIA

Baron Bagge

translated from the German
by Richard & Clara Winston

with a foreword by Patti Smith

*and three letters of Stefan Zweig
and Alexander Lernet-Holenia,
with a note by Arturo Larcati*

A NEW DIRECTIONS PAPERBOOK

Originally published as *Der Baron Bagge* by Paul Zsolnay Verlag, Vienna, Austria. This edition is
published by arrangement with Adelphi Edizioni and the heirs of Alexander Lernet-Holenia.

Manufactured in the United States of America
First published as a New Directions Paperbook (NDP1544 in 2022)

Library of Congress Cataloging-in-Publication Data
Names: Lernet-Holenia, Alexander, 1897–1976, author. | Winston, Richard, translator. |
Winston, Clara, translator. | Smith, Patti, writer of introduction.
Title: Baron Bagge / Alexander Lernet-Holenia, Richard Winston ; translated from
the German by Richard & Clara Winston ; with a foreword by Patti Smith ; and three
letters of Stefan Zweig and Alexander Lernet-Holenia, with a note by Arturo Larcati.
Other titles: Baron Bagge. English
Description: New York : New Directions Publishing, [2022] |
"A New Directions paperbook original"
Identifiers: LCCN 2022028061 | ISBN 9780811234450 (paperback) | ISBN 9780811234467 (ebook)
Subjects: LCSH: World War, 1914–1918—Carpathian Mountains—Fiction. |
LCGFT: Historical fiction. | Novellas.
Classification: LCC PT2623.E74 B313 2022 | DDC 833/.912—dc23/eng/20220613
LC record available at https://lccn.loc.gov/2022028061

10 9 8 7 6 5 4 3 2 1

New Directions Books are published for James Laughlin
by New Directions Publishing Corporation
80 Eighth Avenue, New York 10011

Contents

Foreword

The clarity of love is an unassailable thing, if a thing at all, beyond the norms of logic, immune to the proffering of doubt. Turned like an apple on a stick, the limpid mind is spun in translucent sweetness: love hardens, refusing to crack, and the immortal bride haunts the mortal groom.

An account of such devotion arrives via courier, tied in crimson string. I open the packet hastily and place the pages before me—*Baron Bagge* by the Viennese poet and novelist Alexander Lernet-Holenia—a slim manuscript printed on slightly discolored paper, holding a vague scent of black tea. I know little of the author save that he had served in World War I as a lieutenant in the Austrian Army and was a protégé of the poet Rilke. But I had read his *Count Luna*—a book so astonishing that I immediately reread it, fearful it might disappear—and I had fleetingly wondered whether Lernet-Holenia could marshal such accelerated powers of imagination in another work.

What foolish qualms. Great writers harbor reserves as rich and varied as the caves of Ali Baba. If *Count Luna* might be called a perfectly chatoyant moonstone, surely the work before me would prove to be yet another unimaginable gem. For a poet gives us a verse of unspeakable beauty, only to eclipse it with another, or produce several more in swift succession to form a transporting constellation.

Though not lengthy, this novella, superbly translated by Richard and Clara Winston, begs attentive reading. It unfolds panoramically, as Baron Bagge relates his strange history to his second in an aborted duel, an unnamed but sympathetic listener. He tells a soldier's tale that will twist and couple him forever with the ranks of those in love with the dead.

It is 1915; Lieutenant Bagge has joined the Austro-Hungarian Empire's Count Gondola Dragoons in a brutal campaign against Russia. Forced to retreat, their division flees across the Carpathians to the Hungarian plain. Receiving new orders, they gather reinforcements and head northward on horseback on a reconnaissance mission, surveying the territory. Under banks of low-hanging clouds and through a vortex of storms, they ride at a dizzying pace in an incessant search for the enemy.

Russian forces are sensed, but not seen. The squadron blazes through morphing landscapes into a twilight fringed with ice, a hypernatural world edging the supernatural. Throughout their maneuvers, Bagge is plagued with an odd queasiness, a burgeoning detachment, a sense that another self is navigating in slow motion.

They at last set up camp in Nagy Mihaly, a village intoxicated by revelry. Bagge negotiates his way within a disquieting air of conspiracy, as if everyone is in on a phenomenal universal joke: he alone stands apart, caught in the fabric of a predestined mirage.

The mystified lieutenant is approached by the wraithlike Charlotte Szent-Királys. Beguiled by her eloquence, blue pallor, and golden hair, he allows himself to be drawn into a swirl of festivities. She is pliant in his arms as they dance, cloaked in ecstatic melancholy. The stars, frightening in their brilliance, shift overhead, reinventing time.

As if candlelight were a doctrine, Alexander Lernet-Holenia writes of the grandeur of illuminated halls, the space between realms, the men tramping through the snow in their long brown coats. He notes the burnished braids adorning a uniform, the edge of Charlotte's ivory fan etched with a line from Mallarmé: *With no language, but a beating of wings toward heaven.* He writes of the touch of two hands, of heart chambers entered, one soul pouring into the other.

What happens next does not matter as much as the question that hovers over *Baron Bagge* like a tantalizing mist: how does one distinguish between so-called life and exquisite illusion?

The crimson string unwinds; the scent of black tea surrounds. Time to turn the page and, as a poet might command, tread softly the marbled corridors of an undying dream.

PATTI SMITH
NYC, MAY 2022

Baron Bagge

At a recent reception given by the Minister of Agriculture, a certain Baron Bagge became involved in a dispute with an immature and hot-tempered young man named von Farago. In a voice loud enough to attract everyone's attention, Farago suddenly forbade Bagge to speak with his sister. The Baron asked a major in my regiment, who happened to be present, to be his second; and the major proposed me as the other second. Our opposites claimed that Farago had been justified in protecting his sister since Bagge already had the lives of two women on his conscience. This was news to us. In fact, we knew virtually nothing about Bagge's past as he spent most of his time at his remote estate, Ottmanach, in Carinthia. But we took the position that it was not for us to look into that aspect of the matter. Affairs of such a private character, for which, in addition, there could be no direct proof, were simply not pertinent, we argued. In the end, our view prevailed, and, as custom required, Farago had to make a formal apology. Bagge listened to the apology with a distracted, absentminded expression. Then he bowed, and we took our leave. Subsequently, however, he seemed to feel obligated to make explanations to me, and he told me his story.

Unfortunately, he said, it is only too true that both those unhappy creatures did take their lives. And people say it was on my account. But the truth is I am not to blame. I don't flatter myself that I am particularly good-looking. Nor am I especially rich. And for a long time I had made no efforts at conquest. On the contrary, when I noticed that a woman was beginning to be interested in me, I tried to withdraw and would expressly state that I was not in a position to think of marriage. But apparently these girls were moved by the spirit of contradiction. First one and then the other insisted on marriage, all the more ardently, it may be, because they suspected that I could not marry them at all. You see, I am already married. It happened this way.

When the war started so unexpectedly, I was traveling in Central America—I had wanted to attend the opening of the Panama Canal. I succeeded in returning to Europe on a Dutch vessel and took part in the beginning of the campaign against Russia, serving in the Count Gondola Dragoons. Early in 1915 our forces, retreating under the tremendous pressure of Grand Duke Nicholas' armies, withdrew across the Carpathians to the Hungarian plain. We had suffered tremendous casualties from battle and the hardships of the winter, and some of our units had evaporated. In February, however, they began to be rebuilt. Hordes of fresh recruits, principally from Munkács and Nyiregyháza, were assembled. When the advance was due to start, my division received orders to strike out northward from Tokay on a reconnaissance mission.

Near Tokay, a last spur of the Carpathian Mountains, an extinct volcano, covered with vineyards, thrusts up out of the plain like a muted voice of the underworld. The division, which, in addition to the Gondola and Count Scherffenberg Dragoons, was made up of the De la Ost and the Grand Duke of Tuscany Uhlans, was quartered in Tokay itself and in the surrounding villages. I was first lieutenant in the fourth squadron of my regiment. My captain was a Herr von Semler-Wasserneuburg, and the second lieutenants under me were an American named Hamilton—the United States had at that time not yet declared war upon us—and a very young fellow named Karl Maltitz. The men were mostly Galician Poles, but there was also a sprinkling of Germans and Rumanians from Bukovina. The division was still almost up to peacetime strength.

4

Semler was considered a temperamental, unpredictable character, and there were some who bluntly called him a fool. In any case, life in the small Polish garrisons where the regiment had been stationed for the past several years—a life of boredom and heavy drinking—had done him no good and had apparently stretched his nerves to the breaking point. Besides, he probably carried a hereditary strain of instability. So my mother said, at any rate. She had known the Semlers in Carinthia. It was for my mother's sake that my father, who served originally in the Prussian army, had moved to Carinthia; after his marriage he lived for the most part in Ottmanach. Ottmanach was my mother's property.

Mother knew the Semlers quite well. Wasserneuburg is no more than a day's drive by carriage from Ottmanach. A good many ghost stories about Wasserneuburg were in circulation. Now ghost stories in a family generally mean no more than that the mental condition of the family itself is not what it should be. The story went that mental instability had entered the Semler family in the person of a certain Frau von Neumann. This Frau Neumann, it was said, was the death of five or six husbands in rapid succession, until the last of them finally won mastery over her. I heard this story frequently as a child, but perhaps it was really no more than a nursery tale. Outwardly, at any rate, Semler showed no signs of instability; in fact, he could be extremely charming. But you could never count on him at critical moments.

We were soon to have proof of his unreliability. He was to blame not only for his own death, but for the deaths of Hamilton, Maltitz, and a hundred and twenty non-commissioned officers and men. In fact he came within a hair of bringing about my death also. But perhaps it is not right to place the blame on him. Perhaps his foolishness was merely the instrument of fate, and the disaster into which he led his squadron, the slaughter of so many men and horses, took place in order that something which could no longer happen within the realm of the living—because it was too late—could happen after life.

"In death" is the usual term, but it did not actually take place in death, rather in that time and space which intervene between dying and death itself. For that there is such an interval, many people consider quite certain. According to some it lasts only a few moments; according to others, several days—nine in extreme cases. Hence it is, people aver, that the dead are not buried or cremated until an interval has passed. There have been periods—in ancient Russia, for example—when it was customary to wait more than a week before burying the dead. Besides, what is the real difference between moments and weeks? ... You don't quite grasp my meaning, do you? But I will try to make it clear. Telling you how it all came about will be the best explanation.

I've said nothing so far about Hamilton and Maltitz. Hamilton was, as I've mentioned, an American, from one of the so-called old families in the South. He came from Kentucky, I believe. Or isn't Kentucky in the South? I'm not sure; as I told you, I was in Central America, but not in the United States. Hamilton was tall, bony, and mature beyond his years. Apparently he did not have much use for women. Instead, he drank heavily, and under the influence of alcohol would become amusing. Usually he drank with Semler. Only he could carry his liquor, and Semler could not. Hamilton also supplied the rest of the regiment with excellent whisky, which was hard to come by at this time. He somehow managed to import it from Scotland via Switzerland.

Hamilton was supposed to be quite wealthy. Why exactly he had entered the Austrian army was not clear. Presumably because he was very manly, or had a liking for manly deeds; presumably also because he felt strong ties of comradeship, even for the men

6

of another nation. In any case Anglo-Saxon women are, I believe, such prudes and are also—especially in America—so much after money that it is natural for their men to become manly. Maltitz, however, was not at all manly. He was still a child. And although I never spoke more than a few words with him, I feel sorrier for him than for any of the others. I can still see them all. Semler, on a tall blooded chestnut, his fur collar turned up and laced with gold cord, the looped reins draped over his arm, and his cold hands in his pockets, would stop far up ahead of the squadron and stare broodingly into space. The icy wind at our backs blew the chestnut's tail against its crupper and legs, and indeed it always seemed as if this captain and we ourselves were being blown somewhere by something as invisible as the wind. Hamilton would have his gray, cloth-covered helmet tilted back slightly on his head, the way Americans in late-nineteenth-century prints are shown wearing their top hats. And I can see Maltitz's frozen, childish face and the somewhat dull Slavic peasant faces of the non-commissioned officers and the men in their colorful uniforms, all swathed in furs and parkas, sitting in overladen saddles on horses shaggy with their long winter pelts.... They are all gone, all meeting their end together. If someone wanted to exhume the squadron from the place where it lies, casually buried and rotting, there would be no one missing except me and three or four others; not a man nor horse nor weapon, not a horseshoe, strap, mess-kit, saddle buckle belonging to the squadron would be lacking. But the reality would be no more distinct than my recollection, for it is as if events had engraved every detail into my eyes with red-hot needles. I have forgotten nothing and will never forget, never!

Toward noon on February 26, the squadron was routed out and received orders to advance to the north as a reconnaissance detachment for the division and the army. For in retreating southward our troops had lost contact with the enemy, whose positions were now somewhere between us and the mountains. At the same time a squadron each from the other regiments received orders to proceed similarly toward the Carpathians on reconnaissance patrols, each at a certain distance from the others. The division was to follow soon afterward.

By the time we were mounted, the plain around Tokay was swarming with various formations as the regiments moved out of their quarters and assembled. In the distance individual riders looked like small triangles tilted backward, and since the men wore red breeches, the snow-covered field seemed to be sprinkled with tiny drops of blood. Feebly, like the distant crowing of cocks, the blast of bugles was carried along by the wind.

It was beginning to thaw when we started out, and there were even a few rays of sunlight slanting like brass spears toward the plain. Then the sun disappeared once more, and for the rest of the ride I did not see it again. As the clouds closed, it became somewhat colder. Wisps of mist trailed across the frozen marshes and the Bodrog River. Then the clouds deepened to a woolly, blue-black color. We took it for granted that it would soon snow.

The squadron had left its train and field kitchen behind and was, therefore, overloaded with baggage, provisions, and feed for the horses. We trotted along down the road toward Sárospatak and within a short time passed the spot at the foot of the vineyards where the commander of the division, Field Marshal Lieutenant von Coulant-Kolb, was waiting with his staff. The scarlet of his saddle girth and the scarlet lining of his open coat flashed brilliantly. Suspended from his neck was a decoration. The men of his staff looked spruce and well shaven. The buckles of their horses' trappings gleamed.

The rear area extended as far as Sátoraluujhely, which we

reached by four o'clock in the afternoon. Our ride was without incident, although the road was crowded with artillery and other war equipment. Now, however, we reached the lines stretching endlessly from east to west where our infantry had hastily dug in. And although we heard that there was as yet no sign of the enemy, we were now in territory where he might appear at any moment. Therefore we sent out an advance patrol and flanking units. Then we jumped the infantry positions. Below us, in the trenches, the men were just receiving their evening mess. The field kitchens had been brought up, and the air was filled with the smell of smoke and coffee. Several chevaux-de-frise were moved aside so that we could pass, and we continued on our way. The advance sentries looked after us in silence as we rode into the unknown, in style already belonging to times long past, and in dress and arms equally antiquated. Then the front lines were left behind, and the only signs of life were great flocks of raucous crows flying up out of the wasteland in front of the positions. On our left we still had hills and tawny vineyards, on our right the snow-covered plain out of which rose the windlasses of wells. In the distance, far off to the right, we again saw a small extinct volcano.

Around five o'clock we came up to another of these volcanoes. It was shaped like a blunted cone, was about two hundred feet high, and resembled a small crater on the moon. There was nothing but wasteland all around it. We saw no sign of a village or people. The road, which had been following the railroad embankment, now turned off at an acute angle to the right. Dusk began to descend. The brown wheel ruts in which we were trotting faded into the twilight ahead of us. In snow clouds to the north the Carpathians, themselves like clouds, merged with the dusk.

Our pace slowed now, quite involuntarily. The horses snorted softly and began lifting their legs very high, as though they feared to touch the ground with their hoofs lest something leap up at them. At this point we really should have halted instead of continuing to penetrate unknown territory in the dark. But Semler did not issue the order to halt. Not once did he even turn around; we saw nothing but his own and his bugler's bowed backs as they trotted steadily on. The advance patrol was soon almost invisible up ahead of us. It glided along over the snow, a shadowy group of mounted ghosts. A faint wind sprang up, blowing directly into our faces. Strangely enough, it had an insipid smell, not of snow but rather of unaired rooms and wood smoke. The fancy suddenly came to me—though I was unable to formulate it in any precise way—that the odor of death must be this, or close to it.

I was shortly to be confronted with the origin of this scent. The advance patrol had suddenly come to a stop for a moment. They gave a cry and began to gallop, with raised carbines, toward a solitary tree. Beneath the tree stood three men. That is, from the distance it looked as if they were standing. When we came closer we saw that they were hanging.

They hung side by side from a strong horizontal branch and appeared to touch the ground with their feet. In reality they were not touching it; the wind was making them sway slightly back and forth, and with each swing the branch creaked. They must have been dead for days and have dangled here during thaws, for they exuded that repulsive, sweetish odor we had smelled earlier. Probably they were spies who had been hanged during the retreat. Their hands were tied behind their backs, their heads were tilted, and their half-open eyes peered at us from faces that had acquired an idiotic expression. There was something spongy and amorphous about these bodies; their proportions had oddly changed. The figures looked like assortments of clothing carelessly stuffed with straw—like scarecrows. They wore neither shoes nor boots;

someone had probably donned their footgear and walked off with it. Foxes had gnawed at their feet. Each of them had a scrap of paper pinned to his chest, with some indistinct writing on it. Hamilton struck a match and brought the flame close to the paper. There, as we expected, were the words: "This was a traitor!" Meanwhile, the rest of the squadron had gathered around the tree, and in the flicker of Hamilton's match, everyone looked at the dead men. Under the spreading branches the horses stood as in the roofed arena of a riding school. But after a moment Semler, with a wave of his hand, sent the advance patrol on its way, and the rest of the squadron backed off, formed ranks, and trotted on after the captain.

Full night had fallen, meanwhile, and the hills, obviously covered with vineyards, closed in on the road from the right also. It was altogether irresponsible of Semler to continue riding on. In this terrain we could easily run into an ambush that would cost us all our lives. I made a remark to Hamilton about this and asked him whether we ought not to call Semler's attention to the folly of his actions. But Hamilton growled out in English that we could not stop the idiot, and that if we were fired on we would probably have to turn back.

So we rode on, to the accompaniment of a constant soft rustling and rattle of weapons and equipment. In the distance, a dog began to howl. A second answered it, and then for a while a number of dogs howled. We may have passed by villages, but we did not see them. Now and then lights would bob up and quickly disappear. We no longer knew where we were, for Semler possessed the only map. But we noticed that the hills on our right were now receding again. And the night brightened somewhat; the moon must have risen behind the clouds.

We rode for a good hour and a half more, until we reached

Töketerebes. Here Semler finally decided to spend the night. The situation might well prove to be ticklish; it was possible that we would awaken in the morning to find ourselves side by side with Russians who had also camped for the night in this same vicinity. The village was fairly large and we could not, at that hour of the evening, possibly search the whole place. We had to content ourselves with sending a patrol around the fringes of the village while we ourselves advanced down the village street, half expecting a roar of fire from the houses on both sides. Actually the visibility was worse than if it had been pitch dark. For none of the windows were curtained, and so much light streamed from the houses that we were blinded and literally did not know where our horses were carrying us. In fact Semler, instead of leading the squadron over the bridge which crossed the brook that ran diagonally through the village, had us trotting over the ice of the frozen brook itself. But when they heard us the people soon came pouring out of their doorways. Most of them were Hungarian vintners. Everywhere people were shouting enthusiastically; more and more of the villagers came running up, the men gesticulating, the girls and women smiling at us and handing glasses and jugs of wine up to us. A heady scent like that of a circus rose up from the noisy crowd.

They had seen no Russians, they told us. But there were a good many Slavs living in this vicinity, and some of these might already be on their way to the Russians to betray us. In any case, we took all reasonable precautions. The horses were left saddled, and the men slept dressed and armed. Only a platoon at a time was allowed to loosen the saddle girths temporarily.

We dined at Semler's quarters that evening—the schoolmaster's one-story house. Our orderlies waited on us, and on the whole we were not uncomfortable. But I was still irritated over the manner in which Semler was leading the squadron and during coffee made a remark about it. Semler, who had been putting on a display of charm all during the meal, reacted with an immediate outburst of temper. He had drunk several glasses of Tokay, and these had obviously been too much for him. I promptly rose and left. Maltitz joined me. Semler, too, angrily got up and went out to inspect the defenses. Hamilton, however, remained where he was, drinking whisky and wine; he had two fiddlers playing for him, and the peasants outside squeezed their noses flat against the windows to watch him.

As soon as we were outside, Maltitz struck up a sort of conversation with some girls, although he could not speak Hungarian. Apparently they took a liking to him, and he lingered behind, so that I went on alone to my quarters in a peasant's house. The peasant had drunk himself tipsy, no doubt to celebrate our arrival. He made a long speech to me, of which I did not understand a word. After he had left, his two daughters bustled around my room for so long that I was forced to assume they thought it their patriotic duty, or at least a gesture of that renowned Hungarian hospitality, to entertain me and be nice to me. They were in festival costume, bedecked and beribboned, and not bad-looking. But I was already feeling so strong an evil premonition of what was facing us that I could summon up no interest in them and finally sent them out of the room. I slept very badly; the room was overheated, and I had troubling dreams.

I dreamed that I was attending a variety show in some city. The two peasant girls appeared on the stage and danced a dance with a man who wore a coat of red Chinese silk. The girls' heels gave out a clinking sound like that of spurs, but they wore none. Apparently bells had been built into the heels of their shoes. Then they stepped up on a dais. That is, the girls stepped up on it; the man in the silk coat remained below them, and the girls slipped over the edge of the dais and slowly down into his arms. But suddenly the movement stopped, or rather it became transformed into a swaying and bobbing, and I saw that the girls were dangling from nooses around their necks. But the hanged girls continued to smile. The man below them began taking off their shoes. They went on dancing barefoot in the air. It seemed to me incredible that the audience could go on watching this spectacle, although I myself could not turn my eyes away. But I did jump up to protest—and found myself sitting up in bed as I awoke. Irritable from my dream and from the frightful heat in the room, I got up to go out for a breath of fresh air. At the door, I stumbled over my orderly who lay wrapped in a blanket, asleep on a heap of straw. At the same time the front door opened, and a messenger came in to report that I was to relieve Hamilton, who was on duty.

It was already toward morning. When I stepped out into the street, snow was falling and the wind whistled sharply. I spent some two hours on duty, stumbling around the perimeter of the village and checking the sentries. It was impossible to see two paces ahead. The wind grew steadily stronger, and when we prepared to leave at dawn, it was already a veritable blizzard, the snow mingled with flying sand. When the squadron assembled, one side of horses and riders immediately became coated with snow. The daylight was a bluish white; it seemed to come from everywhere and nowhere at once, pouring down upon us like streams of milk.

We had not yet left the village when we saw Lieutenant Count Chorinski of the Scherffenberg Dragoons coming toward us, accompanied by several mounted men. He reported that he had been assigned to "distant reconnaissance," had been out for three days already, and had spent last night in Vecse. Around five o'clock yesterday evening, he said, he had run into heavy fire from the bridge that crosses the Ondava River at Hór. One of his men had been killed, and he had lost one wounded horse. The road in that direction was undoubtedly blocked by sizable enemy forces; if we wanted to cross the Ondava, we would have to look for another place.

Semler was apparently still suffering from the effects of the wine he had drunk the night before. He snarled at Chorinski that he would take note of the report, but the manner in which he chose to cross the river was none of Chorinski's business. He certainly was not going to run away from a few bridge sentries whom Chorinski apparently took for a whole battalion. In fact, by God, he was going to ride them down.

Thereupon, he turned his back on Chorinski and rode off. We others looked at Chorinski for a moment, and he looked at us; he shrugged and also rode off. "Good luck; you'll need it!" was all he said. We were put to it to keep up with Semler who speeded up to a sharp trot as soon as he reached the outskirts of the village. The advance patrol could barely be discerned in the driving snow, and shortly afterward, when we reached Vecse, Semler pulled them in. "Back!" he shouted. "What's the use of your poking around in this blizzard? I no longer need you. Anyway, I already know where the enemy is." And so we passed through Vecse. Here, too, peasants ran out on the street, hailed us, and offered us wine. But Semler allowed us no time to pause, and outside the village we continued, once again at a fast trot, in a northeasterly direction.

For a while longer I held my peace. Then I suddenly made up my mind and spurred ahead to catch up with Semler. Simultaneously, I saw that Maltitz and Hamilton, as though by prearrangement, had joined me.

Semler, seeing that all of us at once had come up to him, turned in his saddle and surveyed us with raised eyebrows. "Well?" he asked sharply. "May I ask what you gentlemen wish?"

"We cannot stop you from attacking the bridge," I said curtly, "although it is not properly the mission of a reconnaissance detachment to engage in fighting. Actually, we should have reminded you of the regulations yesterday when you insisted on going on in the darkness. ..."

"That's enough!" he bellowed, and his face, partly plastered with snowflakes inside his turned-up fur collar, abruptly took on an almost maniacal expression of arrogance and hatred.

"Very well, very well," I said. "But since the likelihood is that within a half hour you will be lying on the ground, and probably not you alone but most of us, you might have the courtesy to tell us what orders the squadron has received so that someone else will be able to take charge of the survivors—though it may well be just a question of turning around and riding back, after the battle."

Tugging at the gauntlets of his gloves, Semler choked back his rage at this remark and replied: "It is not within the scope of my authority to send back any of the officers who would rather not come along. Otherwise, I would. As matters stand, I have no choice but to take you with me."

I chose not to answer this, and the other two also merely looked at him.

"The orders, if you please!" I said.

"The orders," he shouted into my face, "are these: The squadron is to be led to Nagy Mihaly and is to remain there, send out reconnaissance patrols, and after these have brought in reports to proceed farther north and probe the Laborza Valley. In the right-hand coat pocket of my corpse, you gentlemen will find a map of the Ungvár district. You are to proceed according to that map. Now back to your places."

16

We had no choice but to return to our places, Hamilton and Maltitz to their platoons and I to the rear of the squadron. Of course the order must actually have been: Lead the squadron to Nagy Mihaly *if possible*—not, as Semler had concluded, in any case and at any cost.

The name of the village of Nagy Mihaly, incidentally, although mentioned in so critical a moment, had had a strange effect on me. I instantly recalled all my associations with it, so that for the moment I almost forgot the predicament into which this intemperate commander of ours was about to lead us. Or rather, the name affected me all the more because of the predicament. For in Nagy Mihaly, or Mihalovze, as it was called in the Slavic tongue, my mother had lived for two or three years during her first marriage, while her then husband was commander of a regiment stationed there. She had often spoken of this, and of her friendship with a family named Szent-Király who had lived there. These Szent-Királys owned an estate in or near Nagy Mihaly—I no longer remembered precisely and had myself never met them. My mother, however, had seen them in Vienna shortly before her last illness. At the time they had brought with them an adolescent daughter of whom my mother spoke frequently before her death. In the fashion of old ladies whose minds run constantly on matches, she had remarked that there was a girl I might well marry one of these days; she was already a pretty young thing and would come into no mean fortune. My mother had even hinted that such a marriage would correspond exactly to her wishes. More than once she had maneuvered to have me meet these people, but I either happened to be away from home at the time or displayed no interest at all. At any rate, I never had met them. My mother had often mentioned the girl's name, but I had forgotten it. Then my mother died, and I no longer thought about the family.

Now it all came back to me. My mother's death rose up in my mind again, in all its pitifulness. I saw her as she had been in her last days, curiously shrunken and wretched. I had cherished the hope that there might be a God or, perhaps, some of the ancient gods of our clan, one-time distant relations or sainted ancestors, so to speak, who would receive her well in the place where she was going. Somehow I assumed they would even come forward to meet her, perhaps come right into the house itself, the way relations turn up whenever anything important is afoot: to advise, to assist, or simply to be present. In some such fashion, those mysterious beings might have been on the scene, and in fact my mother's passing took place in the end with so much naturalness, discretion, and serenity that I felt sure she would find the selfsame reliable order of things on the other side as well.

As I considered this, I thought it would be pleasant to convey her last greetings to her friends in Nagy Mihaly. But I had to admit to myself that there was little or no prospect of our arriving there if Semler continued to act as he had been acting. He was now riding along as if he were in a trotting race, and the squadron thundered along behind him in rows of four, at the horses' best gait. What the enlisted men were thinking, or whether they had any conception of what was awaiting us, I could not guess. Those flat Slavic peasant faces betrayed none of their thoughts. Yet, by and by, a curious nervousness swept over the men and horses. There was a sense of mounting tension, as though each of the horses were on the point of taking the bit in its teeth. In particular Hamilton's heavy English hunting mount had become indescribably nervous; it kept breaking into a gallop, and once the American turned toward me and made a curious gesture, pointing at his forehead and shrugging his shoulders. It was not clear whether he meant the captain or his horse. The wind at our backs was sweeping us with great clouds of snow and sand. This might have been favorable for an attack, except that it prevented us from seeing a hundred paces ahead. Bowed forward, heads hunched into fur collars, the mounted men bore forward. All scouts had been pulled in. For a brief while we heard the crackle of rifle fire carried along by the wind from the west. Then that stopped. One of the other reconnaissance detachments must have encountered the enemy and promptly withdrawn.

After a short time the road turned still farther to the right. We were now heading straight toward the east. A little later a long, low symmetrical elevation rose up before us. It was the snow-covered embankment of the Ondava River, whose bed was higher than the level of the plain, and suddenly we saw the bridge close up ahead of us. To the left of it were the few scattered houses of the small village of Hór.

At this moment, Semler ordered a gallop; the squadron, released from the monotonous strain of the ride, stormed forward after him; and almost immediately we heard a few shots fired from directly in front of us. The crack of the rifles was muted by the howl of the snowstorm. I heard the bugler blowing the signal for assault, and the whole mass of cavalry—the men laying the blades of their long, modern English sabers across their horses' necks—thundered forward at their fastest pace. In a few moments, we reached the dirt ramp that led up to the bridge. I saw three or four dragoons vanish from their saddles as if blown away, and several horses also turned head over heels. Snow, stones, and lumps of ice whirled upward and hit me. One pebble struck with a ringing sound against my helmet, the second against my chest, close to my left shoulder. Lucky these are not bullets, I thought. Then the planks of the bridge were rumbling beneath us, and I saw that the Russian guards who had been posted here had been ridden down. In front of us, a few hundred paces away, lay the village of Vásárhely, which had, until now, been hidden from us by the embankments. Swarms of Russians were pouring out of it. Some of them dropped to the ground on the edge of the village itself, some further out in the open fields, and opened fire on us.

But they were already too late. As soon as we had crossed the bridge, we formed a kind of front consisting of scattered groups and clusters. Some of the enemy were still running to meet us; others were already taking to their heels. We rode them all down. We covered the distance to the perimeter of the village in something like half a minute. When we reached the first houses, we cut down the Russians we encountered and drove the rest back into the village. There they threw down their arms and surrendered.

The whole action could have lasted little more than a minute. We had not fully realized that we had been attacking when recall was sounded on the village street. I could no longer remember the various facets of the skirmish; what had happened during the moments of hand-to-hand combat had already slipped my mind. It seemed to me that I had flown rather than ridden to this place. Suddenly I found myself stopping in the middle of the village and was conscious af a tremendous astonishment at being still alive. A cavalry attack against infantry is ordinarily doomed to fail. But this one had succeeded. The enemy had either been sleeping or been completely taken by surprise. Perhaps the Russians had been unable to see because of the driving snow. In any case, here stood the squadron, the horses, with flanks heaving, snorting to catch their breath; and nearby, pressed against the walls of the houses by a group of our men whose threatening gestures made their meaning clear, stood the band of prisoners. The peasants, too, now ventured out on the street and thronged around us with confused shouts. Our losses were comparatively minor. No more than fifteen riders were missing.

Semler waited with averted face until the squadron had assembled behind him. He was once more sitting in his usual careless posture on his chestnut mount, his fur collar turned up and his hands in his pockets, while the wind blew the horse's tail against its crupper and legs. I was compelled to feel admiration for this man who had led such an apparently insane attack with such incredible success.

Now he turned himself and his horse slowly around to face us. I was amazed at the transformation in him. For one thing, he was quite unlike himself in manner, completely calm and composed. His features, tanned by the snow-laden wind—not reddened but tanned to a curious dark shade—betrayed not the slightest sign either of pleasure over the success of the engagement or of triumph that he had been right and we others wrong. His eyes were quite still, almost rigid, fixed upon us without any trace of expression. And the squadron, too, except for the snorting and stamping of the horses, drew up in rows with unusual discipline, without the customary tugging at reins and the almost mechanical cursing of the sergeants. The faces of the men were equally even-tempered, and of the same dark, shaded tan. In general, something had changed fundamentally. The storm itself had suddenly died down, and in spite of the hullabaloo the peasants were making, there reigned a curious, snow-muffled stillness. The peasants themselves sounded as if their shouts came from far off, and then they, too, fell silent. Only the puffing of single gusts of wind over the roofs could be heard and now and then a grating clank when one of the horses ground its teeth against the bit.

Semler gazed at us for several seconds. Then he ordered Hamilton to take his platoon and guard the edge of the village. His voice as he spoke sounded as clear and resonant as the tone of a bell. He instructed Maltitz with his half-platoon to dismount and search the houses. The other half-platoon was sent back to the battlefield to look for our casualties. Finally Semler turned to the prisoners. He astonished me again by the quiet dignity of his bearing as he rode at a walk along the walls of the houses against which the prisoners were standing. It turned out that these men were the remnants of two companies of a rifle regiment. There were three officers among the prisoners. Semler drew up in front of them, and while his chestnut began pawing the snow with a wonderfully graceful movement of its forehoof, Semler asked the officers in French where more enemy troops were to be found. They replied that they would not tell him. "No need, then," Semler commented, after a moment's pause. "I'll see for myself." Once again his voice rang deep and resonant.

Altogether we remained in Vásárhely about an hour. The time flew by for me in a curious dreamlike fashion. I sat mounted in the middle of the village street and was left without any direct orders. One half-platoon was detailed off to return to base to transport the prisoners, conduct the wounded, and carry back a report on the skirmish; but I was not part of this detail, and I felt almost as if I had been forgotten. Moreover, my impressions of what was going on around me did not follow in consecutive order. Rather, it seemed to me, I noticed things at considerable intervals, for each time I made another observation everything was a good deal farther along. I assumed that this odd state of mind was an aftereffect of the danger just past. I was still feeling a strange uncertainty as to whether I had survived the battle. But now I gradually began to recall details of the fighting; in fact, the remembrance took on more vividness than my observations of the present. I clearly heard the chattering of the fire directed against us, saw Russians hobbling off in flight from us, and beheld myself racing into the village. Only then did I really feel that I was here on the village street. I looked around me and saw that the squadron, now only three platoons strong, was on the point of setting off again. The half-platoon with the wounded and prisoners had already left.

During all this time Semler had not spoken a word to me. But just before we started off again, he rode up to me and said: "I must apologize for being so intemperate before. I am sorry about my rudeness, and I would be greatly obliged if you would convey my apology to both the other officers."

"Why," I replied, "I am the one who ought to apologize. And first of all I want to congratulate you on this extraordinary triumph!"

"Thank you," he said.

He looked at me more or less expressionlessly for another moment, nodded, turned away, and rode to the head of the squadron. With a great swishing, as though the horses were stepping through heaps of dried leaves instead of snow, the squadron began to move once more.

Outside the village we headed northeast. Once more we proceeded with strong advance guard. Again there were vineyards to our left. For some stretches the road marched over the hills themselves. To our right, down in the plain, ran the railroad embankment. This was the last lap to Nagy Mihaly. The snow was gradually ceasing. Even back in the village it had been slacking off; now only a few odd flakes still fell. At the same time it grew colder, and the mantle of clouds lifted slightly. But the sun did not break through. In the distance the slopes of the Carpathians were once more visible.

I had assumed that after so successful a skirmish the men

would be in a brighter mood. But far from it. They remained impassively silent. I reported Semler's apology to Hamilton and Maltitz, but it seemed to make no particular impression upon them. Then I began to talk about the luck we had had in the battle. It had really been extraordinary, I said. Strangely, the two of them suddenly averred in an impatient, rather sullen manner that it had not been so extraordinary at all; they at any rate had guessed long ago that it would turn out pretty much as it had.

"I had no such idea," I replied in amazement. But they repeated that they had taken it for granted and been prepared for precisely the outcome we experienced. And when I asked them whether they did not at least find the change in Semler peculiar, they replied that it seemed to them perfectly natural. Shaking my head, I gave up trying to talk with them; in any case, neither of them seemed inclined to continue the conversation. On top of all, Maltitz had the cheek to make a remark which was completely incomprehensible to me. He murmured: "There are some things you can't be told."

"What is that supposed to mean?" I cried out. But he did not reply.

Never in my life had I beheld such ill-tempered victors, and I was especially annoyed by Maltitz' sudden know-it-all attitude and his parroting of everything Hamilton said.

Early in the afternoon we approached Nagy Mihaly. The squadron headed right down the highway, and if the enemy had been anywhere about, we would certainly have been observed and fired upon. But nothing of the sort happened. People did come running toward us from the town itself, however, and in considerable numbers.

Nagy Mihaly is a small town situated half in the plain, half in the Laborza Valley which, at this point, begins to be hemmed in by the mountains. Midway in the valley there juts up a small, but very steep wooded hill, another of those extinct volcanoes that are so common in this region. It is topped by a small church or chapel.

From the foot of this hill, a lane of poplars runs slantwise to the road, and at the intersection of lane and road, right on the outskirts of the town, the townsfolk who had come running toward us stopped and awaited our approach. We also saw an open carriage, presumably a hunting carriage, stop there.

As we came nearer, several of the people waved handkerchiefs to greet us. When we reached them, we stopped to ask whether there were any of the enemy in the town. No, they told us, there had been no sign of the enemy anywhere in the area.

Meanwhile, from the carriage next to which she had been standing, a girl or a young lady in a bearskin coat came up to my horse and asked: "Baron Bagge?" I had no chance to get a closer look at her, for as I bent down courteously to her, to say that I was, her face suddenly moved close to mine; for a moment I looked into wonderful eyes, and then her arms were already around my neck and my mouth was closed by a kiss.

Staggered, I straightened up again, and she, too, took a step back. I now saw that she was tall and exceedingly slender. So light was her stance that she seemed hardly to touch the ground. Her eyes were a radiant blue, as though the whole sky were reflected in them, and they regarded me unblinkingly—like the eyes of goddesses who, it is said, never blink.

"Who are you?" I at last managed to bring out.

"Who am I?" she replied without either smiling or blushing. "I am Charlotte, Charlotte Szent-Király. Don't you know about me? I have heard so much about you." And she added: "I've also seen pictures of you. That is why I recognized you straight off. Oh, I know you well."

So, I thought, this is the daughter of the people of whom.... And my mother had even sent her pictures of me.... "But how do you happen to be here?" I exclaimed. "I mean, how is it you've driven out here? Did you know that I would be coming?"

"Yes," she said. "Perhaps. Perhaps, I really did know. Not that it would be now, not necessarily today. But I knew that you would come sooner or later, Baron Bagge!"

I glanced rapidly at Semler, Hamilton, and Maltitz. But Semler was speaking with several men who were assuring him that the enemy had not yet appeared in these parts at all; he did not look over toward me. And although Hamilton and Maltitz were watching, they seemed not at all surprised by my reception. After a short while they turned their eyes away, without smiling, as though everything were normal, and the men's eyes also regarded me quietly, as if they were witnessing something quite natural and ordinary. Once again the disquieting sensation of dreaminess crept over me, such as had attacked me immediately after the battle. For a moment I doubted whether it was actually myself who sat here. A similar feeling sometimes overcomes us when we are walking, driving, or riding—a dizzying doubt that we ourselves are actually performing these acts. But I attributed this sudden giddiness to overexertion or insufficient sleep.

"Forgive me for being so surprised," I said to Charlotte. "But although when I heard we would be passing through Nagy Mihaly, I made up my mind to visit your family, I never dreamed that you would actually come out to meet me...."

"Oh," she said, "think nothing of it. I often drive out here, stand beside the carriage, and look down the road to see whether anyone is coming. Perhaps I really was looking for you. Are you going to stay in town?"

"Probably. For a while at least."

"My family would be delighted to have you call. Be sure to do so. Wouldn't you like to come to tea with us right away?"

"Today?"

"Yes."

"If my duties permit," I said. "But I really don't know whether it will be possible. We're in a completely exposed position here, and it may be that at any moment we will make contact with the enemy again...."

"Oh no," she said, "there is no enemy around here."

"All very well," I replied. "So we hear. But only a few hours ago we had a skirmish. For that matter, how is it you are still here? Why is it you were not sent to Budapest or Vienna when the Russians approached? I really don't understand...."

"How you keep coming back to the enemy," she said. "I tell you there are none of the enemy around here, and you will certainly not see a single one of them."

"That is just what puzzles me," I said. "By all logic we should long ago have run into more enemy forces."

"Come, come," she said, smiling. "Have you nothing else to talk about with me? Well, I'm sure you'll make up for it at our house—at five or half-past five this afternoon. Until then!"

She waved to me, then turned away, went back to her carriage, and climbed up on to the box beside the driver. The carriage rolled away.

I sat looking after her, still somewhat dazed. The carriage was swiftly lost to view among the first houses of the town. I expected Maltitz or Hamilton to say something, inquire who the girl was, or something of the sort. But they said not a word. They were looking off; apparently their attention had been elsewhere. And now Semler, with a gesture, dismissed the men he had been talking to. The squadron started to move toward the town. But I

27

myself felt strongly that I had to find excuses for the girl, at least to the lieutenants. Heaven only knew what they were actually thinking.

"What do you think of that?" I said.

"What?" Maltitz asked.

"This welcome."

"Well," Maltitz said, "what are we to think of it?"

"It is," I said, "a Hungarian custom for people to exchange kisses on certain formal occasions. People kiss each other especially as a greeting. It's a charming custom. Hadn't you ever noticed it before?"

"Oh yes," Maltitz said. "The men kiss one another, and so do the women. But the women do not kiss the men, at least not if there is nothing between them."

"What do you mean by that?" I said. "This young lady's parents were friends of my mother's."

"Were they?" Maltitz said. "So much the better."

"What is so much the better? What are you getting at?"

"Who me? Nothing."

"Very well!" I snapped.

"What are you making a to-do about?" Hamilton now asked. "We didn't either of us say a word about it."

"No, but I shouldn't like you to misunderstand. Though I, too, wouldn't have thought anything of it if one of you had been greeted in that way."

"Come now," Hamilton said, looking at me with a peculiar expression, "we wouldn't be greeted that way, you know. But it's different for you."

"What do you mean by that?" I exclaimed. "Why should it be different for me? Both of you are behaving very strangely anyway! And saying such peculiar things. What has possessed you two?"

Hamilton and Maltitz looked at one another for a moment. Then Maltitz said: "Nothing. Nothing has possessed us. What gives you that idea? Do you think we have anything against you? Nothing of the kind."

"Yes, something is up!" I cried, slapping down my reins. "There's something funny about every one of your answers. And you especially, Maltitz, have been impertinent beyond belief lately. I won't stand for it. I'm a good deal older than you, and you are obliged to be respectful toward me, understand?"

With that I gathered up the reins again and looked away, acutely irritated over the two men's equivocal remarks and over the fact that they were apparently concealing something from me. I heard Maltitz mutter a few words under his breath but did not turn toward him again. In any case, my attention was diverted by the appearance of the town.

Nagy Mihaly is an extremely small town; never in my life had I seen such a crowd of people in so small a place. As we rode in, they came swarming toward us in hordes, and when we rode into the market square, there was such a mob that we could scarcely make a path for ourselves. I had rather expected to find the place deserted, or almost so, because of the nearness of the enemy. Instead, it was jammed with people. I really could not see where such huge numbers of people found room to live. But as I learned later, most of them had come in from the surrounding countryside. At least so they said. Yet I saw a great many who were unquestionably townsfolk. Some of them I met socially later on. Nagy Mihaly was crammed with government officials and their families, pensioned officers, canonesses, friars, priests, and other religious. In addition, there were the servants of all these people. There were innumerable businessmen, and the land-owners of the vicinity seemed to have nothing better to do than to drive into town continually. Even the peasants and their hired help were swarming in the streets in vivid holiday attire, presumably because they had nothing to do on their farms right now. I wondered where they got all the money they needed in town, for I soon noticed that they did not live at all economically. On the contrary, a veritable mania for amusement, a wild and reckless gaiety sent the people flocking into the taverns and wine-cellars, where they seemed to be raising the roof. I was finally forced to assume that all of them had thronged into the town because of the presence of the Russians; they thought it safer here than out in the country, and they preferred to spend their money rather than leave it to pillagers who might take it all away from them anyhow. But the townsfolk themselves were no less spendthrift; they were throwing their money by the handfuls out of the window. Excess was the characteristic of the town, not only in a qualitative but in a quantitative sense; every single family was extraordinarily large. In addition to children and possibly grandchildren, there seemed to be an incredible number of other relations so that I had to assume that the notorious fertility of the Hungarians did not alone account for it. It was as if nobody died here.

As we advanced into the market square, the mob surrounded us, cheering and waving handkerchiefs. The order to dismount was given, and the next moment we officers were surrounded by crowds of people of approximately our own social class. They spoke to us in the most engaging manner, introduced themselves to us, and pronounced themselves honored if we would care to put up in their houses. They were a little crowded, they admitted, but would certainly find room somehow. They almost fought for the privilege of having us; invitations to dinners, teas, and parties were rained down upon us by perfect strangers. The whole atmosphere had suddenly become completely transformed. There was no longer any mention of the enemy. It did not seem to occur to anyone that the Russians could ever advance upon this town. Instead, the whole populace seemed interested in nothing but welcoming us, issuing invitations to us, seeing that we were properly entertained.

Finding quarters actually proved to be difficult. Hospitable as the people seemed to be, there was hardly room for us all, especially for the men and the horses. This in spite of the fact that Semler immediately sent out a whole platoon to mount guard. Three-quarters of this platoon were dispatched to the northern end of the town, the rest to the Hradek, as the hill with the church was called. From there, we were told, the entire area could be kept under surveillance, even at night; any moving lights, such as might belong to a Russian supply train, would be visible at once. But even the remaining two platoons were hard put to it to find shelter.

We officers as a group finally took up quarters in the monastery. We thought this the best way not to offend the many people who had offered us hospitality, since accepting the invitations of some would have meant refusing the others. The monastery was, so to speak, neutral territory. Moreover, we had more room there comparatively than anywhere else; we were able to stay together and have the squadron nearby, quartered in the various barns and storehouses. Here, too, we had some trouble finding room but finally made satisfactory arrangements.

Meanwhile, dusk was beginning to fall. While there was still some daylight, Semler and I rode on a tour of inspection of the guards at the edge of the town. We also galloped down the lane of poplars to the Hradek, examined the stabling of the horses of the detachment posted there, and finally climbed up to the chapel. The path, zigzagging up the hill under pine trees, was fairly steep and slippery with ice, with stations of the cross along the way. It took us about five minutes to reach the top. In the chapel the men had built a small fire for themselves. The smoke wound its way out through a broken window. To keep the light from showing at night, Semler ordered the windows curtained with the big brown coats the men wore. Bundles of straw for sleeping had just been brought in. The men up here were under the command of a reliable sergeant.

Leaning on the baroque stone balustrade of the narrow balcony circling the chapel, we looked down into the plain below. The view from here was tremendous, in spite of the gathering dusk; it extended northward far into the mountain chain of the Carpathians, which rose like a succession of stage sets one behind the other. We might have seen even farther had it not been for the dense, oppressive sheets of cloud that swathed everything. But we could see the whole of the valley of the Laborza almost as far as Homona. Incidentally, populated as the town itself was, the snow-covered region around it lay completely deserted and lifeless. We saw no trace of human beings, no peasants, vehicles, or troops, not even smoke from the chimneys of the village houses. The land lay unmoving, as though forged of iron. Moreover, everything was still as death; not a dog barked, not a wagon could be heard rattling except in Nagy Mihaly itself. The town was beginning to glow with lights, and a low roaring rose up from it, probably the aggregate of the noise those throngs of people were making.

The sight of this landscape filled me with a terrible melancholy. This feeling was extremely intense, as had been all my feelings throughout the day; I was conscious of a tautening of my nerves, of a sudden dizziness, of the thought that I was dreaming, of bitterness at all the contradictions of the experience. I felt confused, astounded. In fact, I underwent every imaginable emotion except indifference—just as in real dreams there is no indifference, nothing but strong and excessive reactions. Semler, too, stared down silently, utterly motionless, and for so long a time and with, so it seemed to me, so hate-filled a look, that I finally became uneasy. I was on the point of asking him what was the matter when he uttered a low groan, just as if he were writhing on the ground in pain, and stirred at last.

"What is wrong?" I asked.

"Nothing," he replied. But his face was contorted.

"Is something ailing you?"

"No," he said. "Let us go." And he turned away.

I thought he must be having another one of his fits of half-madness.

By six o'clock we were back in town. The streets, although it was almost completely dark by now, were still alive with people. But at least some of the populace had betaken themselves to their houses, from which came shouting, singing, laughter, and a general air of revelry. The peculiarly wild *joie de vivre* of this town continued after nightfall and, in fact, did not cease as long as I myself remained there.

When we dismounted at the monastery, I asked leave of Semler to call on the Szent-Királys. He dismissed me, and I inquired after their house. It was not far. They lived on the edge of town in a house of semi-rural character, something of a country manor. One of our guards, as it happened, was posted at their garden wall.

Here, too, the house was brilliantly illuminated and crowded with people. Two large salons were packed with them. Charlotte received me at the door. She was wearing an afternoon dress, and now I had a chance to see for the first time how incredibly slender she was, especially in the hips. Her face was a little pale, but her lips were rich crimson, though they had not been rouged. The use of cosmetics in those days was not yet common. Her hair was a silky dark blond which looked lighter than it really was; her eyebrows were brunette, with almost a bluish glint. I was struck by the shape of her head; it brought to mind the heads of Egyptian rulers, elongated by the double crown. Perhaps it was Charlotte's coiffure which produced this effect; at any rate, it gave her an air of majesty which united oddly with the trace of childlike obstinacy about her face. When she smiled I saw her teeth flashing perhaps a shade too distinctly; they were of snowy enamel, as in very young animals, and as flawless as the teeth of Greek hetaerae in excavated graves. Altogether, the sight of this unusual young lady set off a host of associations, which at first appeared altogether remote from her but which, it soon became clear, were relevant in their deeper essence—just as everything unusual is full of relationships to other things. The glorious azure of her eyes appeared to reflect vast distances of sky and sea. On the whole, the impression I received was that of a girl enormously superior, in spite of her youth, to the incredibly trivial women of our times. She would have seemed like the reincarnation of some high-born woman of classical antiquity, had not the almost excessive ethereality of her person been so alien to the pomp and glitter of such legendary figures; where classical splendor was a physical thing, hers was a radiance from within. As if through a veil of the dust in which that ancient world had vanished, as if through a puff of ashes from overturned funeral urns, her hair gleamed like an antique fabrication of gold, gradually darkened over long ages.

Apparently I had been looking, or rather staring, at her for an unusually long time, and she must have said something I had not heard or answered. At any rate, I suddenly became aware that she

was smilingly repeating a question: did I not want to meet anyone else here? Accordingly, I followed her, smiling also, though
a little confused. We had to force our way through the throng
of guests. There were groups chatting, playing cards, or taking
refreshments, and in an adjoining room there was music and
dancing, although dancing before dinner was scarcely customary in those days.

First, Charlotte introduced me to her father and her brother,
who was a good many years older than she. The elder Szent-Király
embraced me straightway. He was more than happy to see me, he
emphasized. As he spoke, he kept patting me on the back. "Your
poor mother, your poor mother," he kept saying. She had been
such a dear friend of his wife's. His wife, too, was no longer here,
alas.

"Where is she?" I asked. "In Budapest?"

"No, dead," he replied with a vague expression.

I said I was very sorry.

"Ah," he said, "such an excellent woman. The best in the world.
It's long ago, and yet it seems to me like yesterday that the two
ladies—they were very young, then, of course—were sitting here
in our garden, talking in French, and embroidering petit point or
something of the sort. Your mother," he went on to my astonishment, "was expecting her first child at the time. I can still see
them, both of them. They wore broad-brimmed Florentine straw
hats that shaded their faces. Both of them had the most charming
faces—especially your mother. In fact, I was a little in love with
her.... No, it can't seem that it was only yesterday, because yesterday was a winter day, of course. And it was summer when the two
of them sat in the garden. And, of course, it wasn't your mother
but my own wife who was expecting her first child. Forgive me—
I'm growing forgetful. That's what happens to us when we grow

old; we become forgetful and confuse everything, times and women. Luckily, by the time old age overtakes us, we no longer have wives; otherwise, they would be angry with us all the time. For truth to tell, we are no longer sure who is still alive and who is already dead; we're no longer even sure about ourselves. Other people, of course, don't like to tell us the truth. But let's drop such matters. Let us rejoice instead that you're here at last, even though we needed the war to make you come to visit us. Do I understand that you've just arrived with a squadron? What is this uniform you're wearing, anyhow? The Gondola Dragoons? Funny name. I beg your pardon! How many officers are you? Four? You'll live here with us, of course. I don't understand Charlotte's not having invited you at once! But she is always so shy. Once again, at any rate, I bid you welcome with all my heart!"

And he pressed his slate-gray, warm, slightly damp but well-brushed handlebar mustache against my two cheeks.

"You're very kind," I replied, "but I don't think we can take advantage of your offer; we're already staying at the monastery."

"Ridiculous!" he exclaimed. "Young men taking up quarters at the monastery! You'll be settling down in the cells next, no doubt! No, you're moving in with us, and that at once."

"It really won't be possible," I said. "The men are quartered near us, and because of the nearness of the enemy we cannot…."

"Come, come," he burst out, "nearness of the enemy! I don't know what has got into you people with this enemy of yours. There's no enemy anywhere about. The whole town has been laughing at your posting sentries."

"I beg pardon," I said, "but isn't it possible that the well-known Hungarian optimism may be misleading you into…. It's quite out of the question for us…."

"Nothing of the kind!" he protested. "These are excuses, nothing but excuses. But I refuse to accept them; you're going to stay with us. And if your fellow officers refuse to move, at least they're going to dine with us. Miklós," he went on, turning to his son, "you are to go to the officers at once and ask them here. And have Bagge's things brought over at the same time!"

We left it at that. By the time Semler and the two lieutenants arrived, I had already been introduced to a vast number of people: Zrinyis, Marschallovskis, Leutzendorffs, Türheims, Rabattas, Langenmantels, Halleweyls, and many others. I chatted with them; then I went into the other room with Charlotte and danced with her.

How, I thought during the dancing, can any of this be possible? Night before last we crossed our lines and thought we would see nothing for days but snow and stuffy peasant kitchens. Then for hours we had seen not a soul but the three hanged men; we had spent the night in a village in which I constantly had the feeling that death waited outside; then we had gone through a hard battle which I had thought no more than one out of five of us would survive; then again not a soul to be seen; and now we had come to a town stuffed with people who obviously had nothing but amusement on their minds, where no one talked about the Russians, where a mere mention of the Russians was cause for laughter. The rooms were full of people giving themselves up to mirth, and I was dancing with a girl who was probably the prettiest and certainly the most attractive I had ever seen. She had even kissed me already, in fact right at the start.... How was it all conceivable? I had to admit that the situation had simply bowled me over with surprise; I did not understand it and felt giddy with confusion, particularly when I was so close to Charlotte. She danced unusually well. Her left arm encircled me with a light, incredibly pliant, and hectic vitality. Her eyes, blue as the sea, and above all her mouth were so close to me that I had to make a great effort to preserve my composure. It was a waltz we were dancing; I have no idea how long it lasted, but apparently it was very long, for when it was over we realized that we were the only couple left on the dance floor. Everyone applauded, and Semler, Maltitz, and Hamilton were already there and had been watching us.

I was surprised that Semler had come with the two others and wanted to ask him whether he did not think it necessary to leave one officer on duty. But in the end, I decided not to. I was simply sick of calling his attention to his constant breaches of regulations.

"What were you thinking of while we danced?" Charlotte asked as we returned to our places.

"I was looking into your eyes," I replied.

Shortly afterward we went in to dine.

Two long tables were set in an adjoining salon. There must have been altogether forty or fifty persons present. The meal itself was extremely opulent and very gay; it went on and on, and I asked myself whether this was the usual thing here. If so, the Szent-Királys must already have banqueted away huge fortunes.

After dinner, games and cards were once more played by some, while others danced. Charlotte and I sat side by side on a sofa and watched the dancers.

"Tell me," I said at last, "by what strange chance you came to be waiting on the outskirts of the town and how you recognized me."

She was silent for a moment; then she looked squarely at me and said: "The chance was that I love you."

I had, of course, realized that she was interested in me, but I was so ill-prepared for such candor that I merely leaned forward politely, murmuring, "I beg your pardon?"

"Don't pretend not to know it," she said without embarrassment.

"My dear young lady!" I stammered. "I am certainly honored. But how could I possibly expect such words from you? Besides, that is still no explanation. We have known one another for, at most, six or eight hours, and when you came to meet me outside the town, we did not know one another at all."

"But we did," she replied. "I told you right off that I have known you for a long time."

"But how is that?" I burst out. "You said you had heard about me. So, indeed, had I heard about you. But I must confess that all of my mother's talk did not arouse in me any real interest in you. Of course you did speak of pictures...."

"How odd you are," she replied. "You're looking for explanations for an emotion, as though an emotion were a trivial decision such as at what hour to get up or whether to go for a drive or whether to buy something that takes our fancy. But feelings are not decisions. They arise of their own accord. I told you that I knew you well. My parents used to relate to me many things about you that they had heard from your mother, and they said that your mother also told you about me. I believe they were even thinking of a match between us. And I imagine they went to some lengths to present us to one another in the best light. But none of these things are to the purpose. Their one importance, I imagine, was that I, incidentally, saw photographs of you by which I was enabled to recognize you. But I would have thought about you even if I had known no more than that you existed. Perhaps I would even have conceived of you in dreams if you had never been. Isn't it said that we always dream only of beings who do not exist? So I might have been disappointed when I saw you at last. But true feeling cannot be disappointed by anything, for it is self-engendered and has little to do with the object. You have simply become for me the person of whom I dreamed. You have become that by chance, if there is such a thing as chance. My parents might equally well have spoken of someone else and wished that I would marry this someone else. So you must understand that I was not being importunate when I said what I said a moment ago. It imposes no obligation upon you. And even if you did feel under obligation, you could not do anything for me, even as you could not do anything against me. For every one of us has only himself to deal with; no one can help another person, and every individual, I feel, is alone, utterly alone. I suppose there are no real relationships between human beings. How can there be? We are always only pretexts for one another, nothing more. Pretexts for hatred or for love. But love and hatred arise within us; they operate in us and pass away again solely within ourselves. No real ties link people together. All that we can ever be to one another is a finer or viler pretext for our own emotions. So I was happy when I saw you and liked you, for I had longed for you, and all that I can hope for is that I am not displeasing to you."

I had been listening to this extraordinary girl in great astonishment, and with growing confusion. Was it possible that she was really speaking this way? Were these the words of a girl of eighteen or nineteen? How did she know all these things that I myself had only sensed sometimes, without in the least being able to grasp or express them in any way? The effect upon me was overwhelming. Truth to tell, women need not be intelligent; they need not even be beautiful. If everything this beautiful girl had said had been said to me by another, by someone distinctly ugly, the impression upon me would have been no less. Ah, what women could do, if only they wished it! If they were the way they ought to be and could be, if they followed their inner promptings, if they were not, within themselves, constantly drowning out the voice of the goddess by trivialities, selfishness, timidity, miseducation, and sham, they would long ago have taken their places upon all the thrones of this world, instead of being daily compelled to beg for a pittance of life from equally petty, unpleasant, and small-souled men.

"Charlotte!" I said, at last, and was about to lift her hand, which I held in my two hands, to my mouth to cover it with kisses. "I...."

But she made me stop there.

"Say nothing now," she said. "You must not feel that you have to say something. It makes me happy to be able to let you know how much I love you. What, really, would you want to answer? Leave me now; join the others. Speak with the young ladies, the Langenmantels, the Zrinyis, the Rabattas; amuse yourself with them, so that perhaps you will understand what Charlotte means to you!"

The party went on until two o'clock in the morning. Finally the guests took their leave—the majority probably intending not to sleep, but to go somewhere else and continue their revels until dawn.

By the time we exchanged good nights, we were all somewhat tipsy. Szent-Király insisted on personally conducting me to my room on the upper floor, a fairly showy bedchamber done in red silk and gold. My orderly was there, waiting for me. Szent-Király seated himself on the bed and jounced up and down to test the springs. Meanwhile, he talked steadily. We smoked a few more cigarettes together and had several drinks which he ordered brought up to us. Thereafter he was on the point of sinking back on the bed and falling asleep, but he pulled himself together, stood up, kissed me on both cheeks, and departed.

After he was gone, I myself dropped down on the bed, and my

orderly undressed me. Then he also left. Immediately I had the unpleasant feeling that someone might still come in. So I got up once more and locked the door. Back in bed, I put out the light and instantly fell asleep.

But I could not have been sleeping more than a few minutes when I realized that someone was snuggling up against me.

It was Charlotte.

I could not understand how she had been able to get in through the locked door, especially since the key was in the lock on the inside. I was about to ask her whether this was her habit when guests were in the house, but suddenly I no longer had the strength for such a taunt. She felt like silk.

Had I sent her away, I would probably have misjudged her for ever afterward. As it was, I soon realized how much she really loved me. For this was her first time with any man.

Early next morning Semler detailed three patrols, one under the command of Hamilton, the second under Maltitz, and the third headed by a sergeant. The first was to reconnoiter the Laborza Valley, the second the district toward Fekesháza, and the third in the direction of a mountain called Kiovisko to the north northeast.

I spent the entire day in a dreamlike state of indescribable infatuation with, in fact adoration of, Charlotte. Several times during the day we slipped away from people at the Türheims, where we had been invited to lunch, and the Zrinyis, where we had tea, in order to be alone with one another. Charlotte was an incredibly bewitching and confusing sweetheart. All the while, we scarcely talked with one another; we communicated merely by glances. In spite of the ridiculously large number of people about us, the two of us actually saw only one another.

Toward evening the observers posted on the Hradek reported that during the entire day, they had seen no movement in the

plain except that of our own three patrols. And the patrols themselves, when they returned, could report only that they had nowhere encountered any Russians, nor even any sign of the enemy.
We were at tea when Hamilton and Maltitz entered and delivered
this report.

The utter lifelessness of the region and the complete absence
of Russian forces were incomprehensible to me. I found it, I must
admit, queer to the point of eeriness. Semler, however, flew into
such a fit of rage that he created a great stir; everyone wanted
to know what was perturbing him. When the guests at the tea
learned that this was only another outburst on the part of the
captain "who suspects Russians everywhere and finds them nowhere," there was a great roar of laughter. I simply could not understand this merriment. These people behaved as though there
had never been a war. But strangely enough, even the lieutenants
had made their reports with repressed and distinctly equivocal
smiles, as though they themselves had known beforehand they
would not encounter any enemy. What the devil has got into
those two? I thought once more. Hamilton seemed to have been
infected by Maltitz' impudent and superior manner, so that he
further enraged the captain. Semler soon strode out of the room
and, as I learned later, interrogated the sergeant who had led the
third patrol for a full half-hour, though without securing any
more information than he had already received from the officers.

When Semler returned, he had the map in his hand, and he
issued orders to me in a tone somewhat more controlled, but still
betraying intense agitation:

"Tomorrow morning you will set out at daybreak with your
half-platoon and keep on reconnoitering the Laborza Valley until
you run into enemy forces. You must find them. Be sure you're
back by nightfall day after tomorrow in any case, but I would

not advise you to tell me when you return that you have found nothing!"

This command came as a severe blow to my own hopes, but I had no choice except to obey it. Nevertheless, I did counter: "If there is no enemy around, there is none, though I myself cannot believe there isn't. Still, I'm no magician, and after all it is better, when you consider it, not to find Russians than to run into them and possibly suffer casualties."

That was just about the worst thing I could have said. "We *must* find the enemy!" he shouted, once more calling attention to himself and arousing laughter generally. "We must run into them somewhere. Otherwise we are lost!"

"Why so?" I asked. "Are you afraid of being pensioned off? Or are you determined to get a barony by winning the Order of Maria Theresa? If I were you, I wouldn't get so excited. Sooner or later the division will have to follow us, and then they can see for themselves that none of the enemy is left in this vicinity."

"The devil!" he exclaimed. "The division! The...." But he broke off, angrily waved me away, and turned his back on me.

Whether or not the Russians are around, I thought, Semler, at any rate, seems to have gone off his head again. Still and all I would have to ride out tomorrow.

We spent the evening at the Szent-Királys once more. I told Charlotte that I would have to leave in the morning. She fell silent for a moment, and her brows knitted as if she were in pain. But then she said: "Well, you will be back. But it is a pity to lose the day and the night and the following day. For I'm afraid we will not have many more nights and days."

Whenever and wherever I went, I would come back, I said. But she seemed to have a premonition that all would turn out differently.

Once more the entertainment went on late into the night. Afterward, Charlotte came to me again.

At seven in the morning the following day, I left the town with my half-platoon. The plain lay before us utterly lifeless, and the bank of clouds that veiled the sky was unusually low-lying, gloomy, and oppressive. Moreover, it was thawing slightly. As a matter of fact, the barometer readings during this whole interval, whenever I had the opportunity to observe them in Nagy Mihaly itself, were disturbingly, unusually low. It was almost as if an earthquake were in the offing.

To cut the story short, I rode straight along the river and the abandoned railroad embankment that day, through Homona to the confluence of the Laborza and the Virava. By then we were already deep in the mountains and encountered much snow. Finally we went on all the way to Hegyescsaba. There we spent the night. All this time we had seen no human beings but a few old women who looked like witches, several cripples, and, in Laborzber, a village idiot. The rest of the population had completely vanished. Where they had gone to, it was impossible to discover. Of Russians, I found no trace.

This was utterly bewildering to me, and I racked my brains to account for it. The enemy armies could not possibly have withdrawn, perhaps even retired across the Carpathians, without any operations on our part. And yet no artillery fire could be heard. Nothing. It was uncannily still everywhere, and in Hegyescsaba there was not a soul. Even the stables appeared to be empty. Moreover, it was freezing cold again. We had to break into two empty houses and make fires for ourselves. Then we ate and bedded down for the night, with a strong guard posted.

Next morning it seemed as though the sun were simply unwilling to rise. It was the effect of the mountains, apparently. Darkness lingered for the longest time, and the clouds, or rather the mist, enveloped everything. Finally we set out in spite of this and rode along in a dismal, icy twilight as far as Mezölaborz, where the valley bends off to the right. Here we turned back.

According to the map Semler had given me, we had covered a good two days' march. However, we had seen nothing. It was now eleven o'clock in the morning and we would have to force our horses if we wanted to be back in Nagy Mihaly by night. But the return journey went faster than I expected, chiefly because we had no need to be so cautious as we had been during our forward reconnaissance. Still and all, it was half-past eleven when we reached the town.

We heard that this evening everyone was attending a masked ball at the home of some duke whose name I did not take note of because so many things happened hard upon one another that night.

Semler was awaiting me in the vestibule amid all the raccoon, mink, and opossum coats on the walls. He was pacing up and down, one silver spur jingling—he had kicked the other off. "High time you came!" he burst out.

Upon hearing my report, he had an attack of sheer frenzy.

"Pray control yourself," I said. "Between yesterday morning and tonight, I have ridden nearly a hundred and seventy-five miles, and I am tired beyond words. The enemy simply was not there, and I could not conjure him up by magic. There just aren't any Russians from here to at least the ridge of the Carpathians. Tomorrow morning...."

"Tomorrow morning," he screamed, "we're leaving. I intend to see for myself. That is: we'll start riding out at three. We can just as well advance at night, since there are no Russians in the vicinity, at least according to all your reports. But when day breaks, *I* will find them!"

"I hope you are not questioning the correctness of my report!" I retorted furiously—for on account of Charlotte, I was in despair that he wanted to rush off like this.

"It's my affair what I think of it!" he shouted. "Are you going in at this hour?"

"Of course!" I replied sullenly.

"In spite of how tired you are?"

"Yes, damn it!" I shouted at him.

"If you see Hamilton and Maltitz," he shouted back at me, "you can tell them that the squadron is to be ready at three!"

With that he snatched the map from my hand, took up his fur coat, and dashed out of the building, obviously to issue further orders, although there was plenty of time for that. I watched him for a moment, then turned, cursing under my breath, and went into the next room.

Several connecting salons were completely filled with masked figures. There was an array of costumes, but only period clothes, and of these, most were Biedermeier, a style which I detest. Perhaps for that reason the ball at once annoyed me, quite aside from my being physically exhausted and in an angry, embittered mood. There were comparatively few Empire costumes and almost no baroque ones. On the other hand, there was a swarm of old uniforms, gold-embroidered, government-official frock coats of the last century, chamberlains' regalia, hussars' uniforms, the befurred and bechained capes of Hungarian magnates, and, above all, the white military tunics of the old army. But these were not really white; rather they were yellowed as though they were in reality ancient. In fact it would seem as though all these people had simply fetched their parents' and grandparents' clothes out of wardrobes and donned them. For there were no make-believe costumes, no dominoes, no exotic dresses, so that I suspected the instructions for this ball had been to wear yesteryear's clothes. The floors were strewn with heaps of confetti and tangles of streamers. Everyone seemed to be in fine fettle, and the music was deafening.

I thought I would have difficulty finding Charlotte, but she came to me at once, probably detecting my uniform in the crowd. She was attired in a white Empire dress of astonishing boldness. It was made of almost transparent muslin and left her bosom bare almost down to the rosy nipples of her breasts. Her hair was intertwined with a great deal of jewelry. A fan of pierced ivory set with emeralds dangled from her wrist. She was wearing long, white gloves and sandals of gilded leather over bare feet. She was paler than usual, of a strange, entrancing pallor, in fact, and her face paled even more as she looked at me.

"What is the matter?" she asked.

Only now did I realize that I was still wearing my fur coat, had my pistol strapped on, and was carrying my helmet and riding gloves. My boots, and probably my breeches, were spattered with mud and the remains of dirty snow from the roads.

I hesitated for a moment. Then I said:

"Charlotte...."

"Yes," she faltered. "Do speak!"

"We're leaving," I said. "Tonight—at three." And when she seemed unable to respond, I added: "Of course I saw no sign of the enemy. Now Semler wants to look for Russians himself, with the whole squadron. He's a fool. But he is going, and I...."

"Come," she interrupted, grasping my arm nervously. "It's impossible to talk here; one can't hear oneself think." And she drew me along through the throng. All the while she was growing still paler, if that were possible, and I saw that her lips were quivering. She seemed to want to say something, but I could not make out what. We had to thrust our way through several halls until we came to a less crowded room.

"Well?" she managed to say at last, dropping onto a sofa and unclasping the fan from her wrist. "What does all this mean? You've just come back. How can it be that you're leaving so suddenly in the middle of the night? Need there be this haste?"

"Of course not!" I said. "We could stay on for days, to judge by the whole situation. But Semler seems to think he cannot live without the damned enemy."

"Yes," she murmured, her eyes on the floor. "That seems to be his idea. Everyone says so. But it may really be so."

"What may really be so? There is no enemy far and wide, at least not in the area assigned to us for reconnaissance. I myself don't understand why that is so, but it is. And instead of being glad of it...."

"Semler?"

"Yes, instead of being glad of it, he imagines the enemy must nevertheless be here and can be found. The fool! Apparently he's bent on getting himself the Order of Maria Theresa or some other decoration, or he wants to be made a staff officer, or heaven knows what!"

She was silent and seemed suddenly bereft of strength; her fan, too, as if partaking of her weakness, dropped from her hand and slid from the sofa to the floor. I stooped to retrieve it. In falling it had unfolded and I saw upon it, between the filigree of the ivory sticks and its border of swansdown, a poem traced in gold. It began with the words:

With no language but
A beating of wings toward Heaven …

It was one of the most wonderful of Mallarmé's poems, the one he wrote on his wife's fan in which he says: She stands before a mirror, and with each movement of the fan the mirror brightens up, and with each stroke a little invisible ash trickles in the glass of the mirror.

Avec comme pour langage
Rien qu'un battement aux cieux
Le futur vers se dégage
Du logis très précieux

Aile tout bas la courrière
Cet éventail si c'est lui
Le même par qui derrière
Toi quelque miroir à lui

Limpide (où va redescendre
Pourchassée en chaque grain
Un peu d'invisible cendre
Seule à me rendre chagrin)

Toujours tel il apparaisse
Entre tes mains sans paresse.

I had no idea how this poem came to be upon this fan, but kneeling as I was, I read it to the end—and a thousand times since I have read it on my knees! Then I stood up, folded the fan, and gave it back to Charlotte.

"By whom?" I asked.

But without answering, she took the fan. Then she raised her eyes toward me, and I saw that they were filled with tears.

"If you go," she said, "you will not come back." Her tears, and the tone in which she said this, overcame me.

"What do you mean by that?" I asked. "You know I would come back to you from the end of the world. How can you doubt that?"

"From the end of the world? No," she stammered, "you will not come back!"

I dropped my helmet and gloves on the sofa and seized her hands. "Come, come, what a silly mood!" I exclaimed, pressing her hands. "Why this conviction that I will not come back? Is it some foreboding you have?"

In lieu of reply, she sank sobbing against my shoulder.

"Charlotte," I said, trying to raise her head, "come, sweet, compose yourself. People have begun to look at us. It's nothing. Simply your imagination. What harm can befall me, since we can't even find the enemy? But I don't want you to have the slightest doubts about me. Did you imagine I could leave you without … without your becoming my wife?"

She instantly raised her tear-stained face and looked at me.

"Yes," I said, "I have been wanting to tell you this all along. I cannot help thinking that we are destined for one another. And as you know, our parents would have rejoiced in our union. At least my mother openly expressed her hope that this marriage would come about. I intend to speak to your father at once. Where is he? Is he present? We'll go to him at once."

"Oh," she sobbed, "it isn't that.…"

"But it is all I can do to prove to you what you mean to me," I said. "You know I love you, Charlotte! I love you more than my life."

She clung to me with her arms around my neck.

"Better death with you," she wept, "than living without you. But what will death be like without you?"

"Charlotte," I remonstrated, "what is this you're saying? Are you really anxious for me? I tell you, there's no cause to be. What does all this amount to? A brief separation, for a few days, a few weeks at most. So many men have gone away and returned again."

"But not you," she sobbed. "You will never come back again!"

"Come now," I said, "don't fill your mind with imaginings!" And I stood up, drawing her up with me. "Come," I said, "we have no more time to lose. Let us go to your father at once."

I shall pass over Szent-Király's noisy emotion when he heard the news. His arms in his lavender dress coat flailing like the vanes of a windmill, he instantly seized the occasion to draw me to his heart and press his tear-drenched mustache against my face. "Ah," he kept repeating, "if only the ladies had lived to see this moment!" He meant his wife and my mother. His one disappointment was that the wedding would have to take place so precipitately. I am sure he would have preferred a vast affair with hundreds of guests and feasting for days. As it was he wanted at least to invite the guests at this ball to the wedding. With difficulty I managed to dissuade him. Finally we agreed that only the close relatives of his family and Hamilton and Maltitz as my own best men would be present. Charlotte's brother was dispatched to bring the priest.

(This brother, Miklós von Szent-Király, figures in my memory only because of the conscientious way he carried out the occasional commissions given him by his father. For himself he was apparently interested in nothing but agriculture, talked scarcely at all, and gave the impression of being tired and sleepy. Only when he was given orders to do something did his eyes light up like those of a peasant who is receiving some specific directions.)

I set out to hunt up my two lieutenants and soon found them chatting with a group of young ladies. That is, Maltitz was conversing in his new, urbane way. Hamilton merely stood by silently, draining glass after glass from the silver tray a servant was holding. When the two saw me coming, they grinned and called out: "Well, have you found the whole Russian army?"

"Jest away," I answered. "Of course, I didn't find anything. Nevertheless, we're riding out again this very night, at three o'clock."

They would not believe it.

"My word of honor," I said. "But first I'm to be married. I am taking Fräulein von Szent-Király for my wife. You two have acted rather oddly toward me of late, but in spite of that I want to ask you to be my best men."

Instead of replying, they once again threw peculiar, meaningful glances at one another.

"There you go again!" I burst out. "Do you want to be my best men or not?"

"Of course," they now said. "And heartiest congratulations."

For the next hour the whole horde of people attending the ball thronged around Charlotte, Szent-Király, and me, congratulating us, and Szent-Király responded to all these effusions by pressing that handlebar mustache of his against the faces of all the men and most of the women, the younger women, at any rate. Meanwhile, we were being steadily plied with wine and champagne. It was two o'clock before we went over to the church, followed by most of the guests.

The wedding developed into one of the strangest scenes I have ever witnessed. In the great vaulted nave, illuminated by only a few candles, the company assembled, talking in whispers, glittering with jewels, flashing gold and silver embroidery, their fur coats imperfectly covering their masquerades, while the priest intoned the marriage service. So bizarre and ghostly was the sight that one was led to think the spirits of the dead were in attendance, clad in the apparel of their lifetimes. At last the priest joined Charlotte's hand with mine. That touch was all we had of wedding night. But never, I fervently believe, have two souls been more closely united than were ours at that moment. My heart became Charlotte's and hers mine for all time and all eternity.

Then Szent-Király boisterously blew his nose, and a general sneezing and wiping away of tears seized the entire crowd. One by one the people came up to wish us joy. The next step was to hasten to the monastery where the squadron was already assembling.

Charlotte, with a fur mantle thrown over her scanty evening dress, walked beside me through the snow almost barefoot in her thin gold sandals, and the others followed. We walked slowly, our hands still interlocked, but we were unable to say a word to one another. As we drew near, the glittering double file of riders loomed up before us on the snow. Horses tossed their heads, and weapons clinked softly. Semler, who was standing in front of the squadron, beside the bugler's horse and his own, came toward us, helmet already on his head, and offered us felicitations.

"I am sorry I was unable to be present in the church," he said to me, "but I had arrangements to make. I also sincerely regret that I cannot let you remain behind for a short time. But the situation will not permit it. I apologize to you also, Baroness," he said, turning to Charlotte and kissing her hand. Thereupon he bowed to us and the others and stalked back to his place, dogged by the audible disapprobation of the wedding party. Remarks were made that his courtesies were a bit tardy. The assembled townsfolk plainly indicated that they thought this abrupt departure sheer foolishness.

However that might be, there was nothing for us to do but bid farewell. For a few moments I looked at Charlotte; then I took her in my arms and kissed her for the last time. Since the wedding ceremony, she had not spoken a word. She was no longer weeping, and now she merely stared fixedly at me, her wide-open eyes unnaturally still, as though all bliss were at an end. It struck me that she no longer had the strength even to respond to my kiss. Her mouth felt lifeless. I was afraid this parting would be too harrowing for her and turned quickly away. While I shook hands with Miklós, I felt for the last time Szent-Király's mustache against my cheeks. Then I freed myself, took the ten or twenty paces over to the squadron, and quickly mounted. Hamilton and Maltitz had come with me and also swung into their saddles.

During the half minute that passed before Semler and the bugler also mounted, there was dead silence. From my saddle I tried to peruse Charlotte's face, but could see only the white gleam of it and the pallor of her dress as she stood, coat ungirt, between the dim figures of her father and her brother. Behind them stood the shadowy crowd of townsfolk.

During those seconds it seemed to me that I had lived here for years rather than days, and that it would be wholly impossible for me henceforth to live anywhere else. But at the same time I, too, was swept by the anguished presentiment, by a virtual certainty that I would never return here. It was not the idea that everything would be different when I came back—as things always are different when one returns—but that I suddenly knew with absolute certainty that I would more easily reach the moon than come back. I knew that there was simply no returning, not to this place. Whatever I left behind was gone. Never would I return, never again.

In a sudden access of mental turmoil, shaken by dread and confusion, I had the impulse to leap from the horse, rush up to

Charlotte, seize her in my embrace, and rather suffer myself to be killed than taken away from her. But at that moment Semler gave the order to start. That is, I did not hear the order, but I saw the captain make a bound to the right. By fours the riders wheeled after him, and the squadron thundered down the road toward the north, carrying me along with it.

As though the spell which had been upon me and everyone else had been broken, loud cheers and shouts rose from the hitherto silent crowd, and hands waved frenziedly after us. I turned once more to look for Charlotte. But something like a veil of nocturnal snow or ashes was drifting between myself and her, and I could not see her.

Thenceforth our ride continued for another three days and a few hours of the fourth.

I do not intend to relate the particulars of this part of our expedition. For that matter, they are extraneous to this tale. I need only mention that by nine o'clock that morning we were in Homona where the valley of the Laborza branches off in a northerly direction from the valley of the Csiroka. I assumed Semler would continue advancing up the Laborza, but instead he turned almost due east into the other valley. When I remarked upon this, asking why he was not heading north, he murmured: "There's nothing in that direction. You, yourself, said so." From then on he displayed a tendency to avoid the northern direction whenever possible. It was almost as if he feared it, and he constantly invented excuses, which he brought forth in a more or less indistinct mumble, for evading the squadron's actual orders.

In the course of the next three days we passed through Sinaja, Taksány, and Nagy Polány, constantly moving into the mountains and finally following wheel tracks that led through a pass and into the valley of the Zolinka. We cut through that valley also and proceeded over pathless highlands where the horses had to plow through deep snow. By evening of the third day, just as dusk was falling, we reached the valley of the San. During all this time we had encountered no sign of the enemy, and from Sinaja on no human beings at all. All the villages were deserted; the inhabitants had evidently fled; and there was no one about even to tell us where they had gone.

Moreover, the mass of clouds, which hid sky and mountains, grew steadily denser. In the end it became a kind of blackish fog through which we groped our way. Daybreak was delayed by more than an hour, and twilight fell an hour sooner, although twilight could scarcely be said to differ from the gloom prevailing through the day. In addition it snowed. But what came down seemed to be stringy fragments of mist, as though we were under a rain of ashes. Even the color of the falling flakes was grey, as if this were not snow but ash from one of the extinct volcanoes awakened to new life. To make matters worse, our rations of meat gave out on this third day, so that it should have been an occasion for rejoicing when Hamilton killed a stag. This stag, which had already lost its antlers, unexpectedly turned up in front of us, stared at us out of completely expressionless lifeless eyes, like an animal already dead, and then clumsily and heavily took flight. Hamilton pursued it on his horse for a short distance and finally brought it down with several shots from his big American revolver. However, I refused to eat the meat of an animal so obviously sick. The others had no such compunction and maintained afterward that although the meat was tough, it tasted strangely of fragrant herbs.

Next morning, incidentally, I had another demonstration of Hamilton's skill as a hunter. We had spent the night in the meager shelter afforded by tumble-down shacks close by the bank of the San. When I stepped out into the tardy, disheartening dawn of another of those belated, dreary days which so closely resembled the nights, I saw Hamilton stealing about under the nearby trees and peering up into their leafless branches. He was carrying a long, pole-like weapon. To my amazement it turned out to be an extaordinarily old-fashioned, excessively long-barreled rifle. When I asked, he explained that this was called a Kentucky rifle. He had brought it from home, he said, and always carried it with him. But I could not imagine where he had kept it up to now. Certainly not on his horse, for it was taller than a man, and I was sure I would have noticed it long ago. But I had no time to puzzle my mind any further about this, for Hamilton placed the exotic muzzle-loader against his cheek and fired a smoky blast into the branches of the trees. Two wild turkeys promptly fell at our feet, flapped their wings for a little, and lay still. I could not believe my eyes. Impossible, I thought. This simply could not be. For in these parts, there were no wild turkeys of any species that lived in trees. I thought I must be dreaming or out of my mind. But Hamilton, with perfect calm, hung the birds from his saddle and mounted his horse.

Immediately afterward, the squadron, which had meanwhile assembled, started off. Our course now led downstream and straight north. Semler had apparently lost his distaste for that quarter of the world, or else the topography of the valley was forcing him in that direction. The San roared on our right, so loudly that it sounded as if shards of glass rather than water ran in its bed; a tremendous grinding and clinking rose up from the river. The further we advanced, the lower the valley floor dropped, while at the same time the mists swathing the mountains became more translucent and we saw that the peaks, riding rockily out of gloomy forests of tremendous pines, had risen to meet the sky and scarcely admitted the daylight any longer. Only far up at the top, among the rocky ridges, was there a single streak of silver-colored light. Hamilton grinned and said in English: "Every cloud has a silver lining." Here below in the gorge, however, day had once more been changed into night. But from the bed of the river a strange glow rose up to us, something like the ocean's phosphorescence, and now the ground itself began to shine as if it were strewn with phosphorus; even the riders and horses emanated an unnatural light, or rather they were surrounded by a luminous mist as though a candle were burning behind each man. I observed all these phenomena with indescribably tormented sensations. I thought I was suffering from a nightmare, and as in a dream, it suddenly seemed impossible for me to move, speak, or shout; rather I slavishly followed the procession of the others without taking any action of my own, though I constantly wanted to ask them what all this madness meant. But I could not speak a word, and they rode on with measured pace as though they noticed nothing and were surprised by nothing.

Meanwhile, on the road ahead of us, there suddenly appeared a powerful metallic glitter, and as we drew nearer I saw that it came from a bridge which at this point crossed the river. There was a tremendous roaring, as from heaven-high waterfalls of glass, and steam, as if from intensely hot waters, rose in all colors of the rainbow from the deep cleft of the stream. The bridge itself was covered with sheets of metal that gleamed like gold. Why, it was gold with which the bridge was sheathed!

This could no longer be reality; this must be a dream, although I could not imagine when and how it had begun. No bridges are sheathed with gold! With incredible effort, by the most frightful exertion of all my strength, as though my muscles were going to tear apart my jawbones, I succeeded at this extreme moment in opening my lips and moving my tongue. "Where are you going?" I shouted into the roaring of the cataracts. "Are you riding…are you riding across the bridge?" "Yes," they all answered, and their voices rang like a choir of bells, "we are riding across!" And the hoofs of the horses touched the bridge and sounded like golden thunder.

But I, I wrenched my horse around and spurred to one side, while in my mind I shouted: I am not riding with you, I don't want to cross, I don't want to, this *must* be a dream, but I want to wake—and I awoke.

I lay in the middle of the bridge, but of course it was not the bridge of gold that led across the roaring river. It was still the bridge at Hór, the bridge over the Ondava, across which Semler had led the attack (eight full days ago, as it seemed to me, but in reality, merely a moment ago). The two stones which had been kicked up by the horses as we stormed the embankment had not been pebbles, but bullets, and they had thrown me from my horse. I was bleeding from a wound near the temple, and the left side of my chest, rather high up, had been pierced by a bullet. In falling I had fainted, but my unconsciousness could not have lasted longer than a few seconds. For the golden thunder of the heaving and throbbing plates of the bridge across the river of glassy water was still ringing in my ears, but it was only the thunder of the wooden bridge of Hór which crossed the Ondava. The planks were still rumbling and vibrating from the hoofs of the horses that had just dashed across them, but neither horses nor riders were to be seen. In the course of a few seconds, the squadron had vanished, been extinguished, been swept away by the raging, howling fire that was still roaring over my head. The squadron lay on the ground; the attack, as could have been foreseen, had failed completely, and hordes of Russians in earthen brown coats were running out of the nearby village and spitting the wounded men who still stirred upon their long bayonets. Enemy artillery now also spoke up, and I recognized the shrieking blast and the poisonous, pitch-black smoke of Japanese shells. A single non-com and three or four dragoons, who were riding with me at the rear of the squadron, had had the chance to wrench their horses around while they were still partly covered by the river embankment. They had sprung from their saddles and were now dragging me back to safety. As they started lifting me on to one of the horses, I lost consciousness again.

It was many days later before I awoke for the second time. I was in bed in a military hospital in Hungary. But it took me weeks, months, possibly years, to realize that everything I had dreamed during those seconds when I lay on the bridge had been in fact nothing more than a dream. To this day I cannot fully believe it, unless it may be that if death is a dream, life, too, is merely a dream. But between these dreams bridges lead back and forth, and who may truly say what is death and what life, or where the space and time between them begin and end?

In the hospital I lay motionless with ice packs on my lung wound, forbidden to speak above a whisper, and slowly, very slowly recovered. The volunteer nurse assigned to me was an old spinster, a member of Hungarian society, who knew everyone and everything. To keep my mind occupied, she told me stories by the hour, although I was not permitted to reply to her. Before long I knew all the gossip of Hungary. But whenever she paused long enough to inquire whether her tales were boring me, I would blink a "no" with my eyes. I kept hoping that sooner or later she would come around to the subject that most concerned me; for the sake of that I willingly listened to everything else. Finally she did begin to speak of it. Without suspecting my connection with the Szent-Királys, she mentioned them also.

Charlotte Szent-Király had been dead a long time, had long

61

been dead at the time I dreamed I met her. Circassians, come on a plundering raid across the Carpathians, had killed her, her father, and her brother when the family refused them tribute. Only the mother (who according to Szent-Király had passed away) was still alive; she was living in the capital.

Altogether, it seemed that I had dreamed solely of the dead. I suspect that I saw no living persons in my dream. That accounted for the apparent emptiness of the country during our ride—in actuality the entire region must have been swarming with Russians at the time. That accounted also for the crowding in Nagy Mihaly, where all the shades had congregated, as it were; that accounted for my days of reconnoitering with the squadron which perished even while I was dreaming of it. Only Semler kept looking for the enemy. For he imagined that if he could still find the enemy, he was not dead. He went on the nine-days' wandering of the dead that is prescribed in myth; he drifted toward the dreamland, rode north to the bridge of Hór or Har where the road to Hel begins, to the bridge of gold that leads into the irrevocable from which no man returns. I alone had been able to turn around and come back. For it is said that if anyone turns around on the road to death, he will come back.

Long after the end of the war, I went by car over the route I had traversed in my dream. It was not too different from the dream road, which I had apparently constructed after a map I had studied and odd bits of knowledge about the region. For in extreme situations the human brain and nerves can operate with a keenness a thousandfold greater than normal, so that we attain an almost godlike prescience. But on the other hand, in spite of similarities, the real terrain was altogether different. The bridge at Hór where I had hovered for the fraction of a minute between life and death was, to be sure, exactly as it had once been. Only now herds of cattle were grazing on the meadows round about, and on the other side of the bridge was a huge mound of earth heaped up like a tomb for prehistoric heroes. Beneath this mound lay the squadron, the hecatomb, the dead hundred, which in the number system of northern lands is a hundred and twenty. For on our heels, in the course of the advance which ultimately resulted in the conquest of all Poland, our army had followed and had buried the dead, the heroes—everyone who is dead is a hero in some sense. Even Semler was a hero, for all his mad folly.

I went on to Nagy Mihaly. This town, however, was in no respect the town of my dream. It proved to be a small, petty, dreary, provincial place. The countryside round about, on the other hand, was swarming with peasants. The Szent-Királys' home, although I found it again without any difficulty, bore no resemblance to the country manor I remembered. I wanted at least to be shown the house where my mother had lived. But no one knew any longer where that had been.

Finally, I wanted to see Charlotte's grave. It had been neglected and was overgrown with tall grass and pale blue larkspur. I stood by the grave and curiously enough felt nothing. It was as though a total stranger were buried here. And I suppose it was in truth a stranger.

When I turned to go, I saw a well-dressed man of about forty standing at the entrance to the cemetery and staring at me. I decided that he must be one of the Szent-Királys, or one of their kinsfolk who now owned the estate, and that he had been told someone was inspecting the family graves. He had probably hurried out here to talk with me and perhaps to apologize for the condition of the graves; for he seemed to be expecting criticism and looked down at the ground when I drew near. But I went on past him without a word. He interested me no more than the alien grave.

And so I drove farther on into the Laborza Valley. It was flat and pleasant country, by no means gloomy, and the valleys farther northeast and north were nowhere hemmed in by sky-high mountains or filled with black fog like the smoke of bursting Japanese shells. I was unable to find again the place in the mountains where Hamilton had shot the stag, although I covered that area on foot. On the other hand, I did come upon the bridge where our journey had ended, the bridge of gold across the river of glass. Naturally the bridge was made of wood, and only water, not glass, flowed in the San River. But several workmen were engaged in repairing the bridge, so that it was once more impossible for me to cross it. I sighed with relief. For even had the workmen not been there, I probably would not have had the courage to pass over that bridge. Whether it was truly the bridge coated with beaten gold over which the hordes of dead men had ridden by the hundred, or the Arabs' bridge of Al-Sirat, narrow as the blade of a sharpened scimitar, which leads to Paradise, or whether it was merely the simple wooden bridge across the San—in any case, I fear, I could not have forced myself to set foot upon it.

For the truth is that in spite of my dislike for fantasies, deep within me that dream is still reality and reality seems no more than a dream. And no matter how often I may be told that Charlotte Szent-Király was, in fact, dark-haired and by no means especially pretty, though certainly not ugly, she remains for me the girl I have always dreamed of, the bride who has ever waited for me, the maiden whose sacred head gleams like a goddess' through death's rain of ashes, through the silent, trickling mist of ashes that fall from the volcanoes in the realm of the dead; she remains the one woman, unique and radiant, transfigured and indestructible for all eternity.

Three Letters

from the correspondence of Stefan Zweig
& Alexander Lernet-Holenia,
with a brief note by Arturo Larcati

translated from the German by Krishna Winston

Stefan Zweig to Alexander Lernet-Holenia

Vienna, Hotel Regina [1936]

Dear Lernet,

In the midst of all the annoyances with which these times are showering me, I must pause to acknowledge a rare and special pleasure. Your *Baron Bagge* is a masterpiece! It is positively *magical* the way dream and reality glide seamlessly into one another, creating a realm of visionary luminescence, a visual plenitude whose color derives from fever and coursing blood: you wrote this novella in a state of heightened inspiration such as I have seen otherwise only in your poems. The one work with which I can compare your masterful prose is Hofmannsthal's *Andreas*. Because, as you know, I feel so close to you as a friend and fellow human being, I find it particularly gratifying that you, and you above all, have created this flawless chef d'oeuvre, in which every word and every sentence rests lightly right where it belongs. Truly you wrote this unforgettable novella in a state of grace.

The times are driving me hither and yon. In the course of the summer I shall probably make my way to Brazil. How I should have liked to have shaken your hand once more before leaving!

With warmest wishes,
Stefan Zweig

Alexander Lernet-Holenia to Stefan Zweig

St. Wolfgang, June 23, 1936

My most dear and esteemed Dr. Zweig,

Thank you so much for your beautiful and generous letter. I am especially pleased that no recent developments have been able to weaken the bonds of friendship and intellectual affinity between us, and that I keep having occasions to tell you how much I respect, admire, and esteem you. Today I am somewhat under the weather, but I should not like the day to pass without my replying at once to your message. To be sure, it is impossible to say in a letter all I might bring up on the subject of *Maltravers* and *Bagge*. You see, the contrast between these two books increasingly strikes me as problematic. In *Maltravers* everything seems to have been said, and none of it skillfully. In *Bagge* almost everything is executed skillfully, but actually nothing is "said." Perhaps the truth is that one cannot "say" anything—unless it expresses itself. Yet the author's heart clings to what is more incomplete or unfinished, while he remains largely unaware of what has been achieved. That was my experience with *Bagge*. I was taken aback when the book received so much praise.

By contrast, the *content* of *Maltravers* seemed to have meaning for very few, and the form often came in for criticism. Perhaps *only* form really matters, to the extent that it gives no clue as to what was originally formed, or allows no one to discern that. Or perhaps it makes no difference *what* is formed. The shape and configuration seem to be all, and the *content* carries weight only if it has become *meaning* …

In the case of *Bagge*, I really did not know what I was writing. Viewed superficially: the myth of the nine-day journey toward death. But the book's essence seems to lie elsewhere, and I, who wrote the book, still cannot put my finger on it. Actually this is a tragic situation: that even in this most intellectual of professions one's individual personality has as little influence as is increasingly the case in other contexts; that just as someone else rules over us, "something else" writes our books. Not we ourselves. Recognizing that has to make us very, very humble. For perhaps—if one pursues this thought to its logical conclusion—Luther and Calvin had it right more than Erasmus and Castello: a devastating realization. So why are we here? As artistic instruments for the energies of others, whether these energies reside in reformers, in dictators, in the people, or in God? Never, so it would seem, are we the authors, only the scribes. —

Dear Dr. Zweig, do not go to Brazil; there [added in the left margin, at a right angle to the body of the letter:] you will find only a random assortment of people who instead of doing real work just form a club and blather endlessly. Nothing ever comes of it: all these Pen Clubs and cultural unions and the like accomplish nothing. But if you do go, I wish you a lovely crossing, and I hope we shall see each other again in the fall. In the meantime, I remain, ever grateful,

> Your faithful and sincere
> Alexander Lernet

Alexander Lernet-Holenia to Stefan Zweig

October 8, 1937

My dear and esteemed Dr. Zweig,

Thank you so much for your gracious letter; I was so happy to receive it that I am answering right away to thank you. I especially regret that we see each other so seldom. You have accompanied me so kindly, with such true friendship, through much of my life, especially during the time when a person's sensibilities are more acute and beautiful than later on, when, like an atomized droplet of soot in the air we breathe, a dusky trace begins, at first unnoticed, to deposit itself on our hands and our heart like crepe, until our eyes grow dimmer and our feelings more self-centered, and our feet eventually grope only for those "silent stairways" that lead downward! And we have reason to suspect that this is befalling not only our life but also our whole world.

For almost a year I have done no work, and now I sit here dreamily—too dreamily—with the manuscript on my desk of a comedy that bores me, and my thoughts wander to entirely different subjects. Recently, visiting friends in Holland, I picked up your Erasmus—again. It is an incredibly true book! It is your most personal book, and at the same time the most apt book for our times.

I am looking forward greatly to your work on Magellan. Don't all of us wish, now more than ever, to seek out, with a "sourire du pâle Vasco," as Mallarmé put it, oceans that have not yet been traversed. But there are none left.

In two weeks I shall travel to Paris for two or three days—but I fear there will not be time for me to hop over to London.

So I am left with only the hope of seeing you again here. This hope, however, is more fervent and heartfelt than ever!

Your most sincere
Alexander Lernet

* * *

A *note*

The three letters reprinted here—one from Stefan Zweig and two from Alexander Lernet-Holenia (1897–1976)—document a friendship between two writers who could not have been more different in age, temperament, and writing style, but who evidently maintained quite a close relationship for many years. Sadly, as only one of Zweig's letters to Lernet-Holenia survives, the correspondence reveals the friendship primarily from Lernet-Holenia's point of view.

One can only speculate as to why Zweig's letters seem to be lost for good. Perhaps they went astray in the course of a move, or Lernet-Holenia destroyed them himself to erase any traces of his "apprenticeship." In view of the fact that he even destroyed letters from Rilke, that would not be inconceivable. What is certain, however, is that when Zweig left Salzburg in 1934 he did not burn Lernet-Holenia's letters, although he did burn many other letters and manuscripts that he did not want to take with him into exile. So we can conclude that the friendship meant a great deal to him.

These three letters offer insight into the literary dialogue between the two writers; each mentions the other's work and comments on it effusively: Zweig expresses his admiration for the novella *Baron Bagge*, and Lernet-Holenia speaks enthusiastically of Zweig's biography of Erasmus. Their mutual admiration emerges unmistakably from the correspondence. Lernet-Holenia also uses his letters as occasions to reflect on his own art.

Stefan Zweig clearly played the role of a mentor or advisor to the other writer, sixteen years his junior, and put his excellent relationships in publishing at Lernet-Holenia's disposal. Under the circumstances, it comes as something of a surprise that the younger author manifests such a sense of his own worth and such self-confidence in his interactions with his older, very successful colleague. Whereas Zweig did not consider himself a full-fledged writer until his drama *Jeremiah* (1917) had appeared, Lernet-Holenia expressed complete confidence in his own abilities from the outset.

The letters offer some glimpses into the private life of Lernet-Holenia, who "painstakingly erased almost all traces of his biography."[1] We learn, for instance, about his visits to Zweig in the little Paschinger Palace in Salzburg, and about Zweig's visits to him in St. Wolfgang. Other meetings in Berlin and Paris are documented—further evidence of quite a close friendship.

The correspondence also captures a "conversation about poetry"—Lernet-Holenia's favorite genre. Several times the younger man shares samples of his work with his friend. Stefan Zweig held a high opinion of the poems' quality. In a 1935 letter to Joseph Roth, for example, he bases his approval of Roth's choice of a new publisher, Herbert Reichner, on Reichner's excellent list, which includes Lernet-Holenia's poetry.[2] In 1939, when Zweig is advising the British Germanist Jethro Bithell on an anthology of contemporary German verse he is putting together, Lernet-Holenia is one of the poets Zweig urges Bithell to include, along with Max Hermann-Neisse.[3]

In 1935, when Stefan Zweig is considering ending any future collaboration with Richard Strauss because of the outcry against a Jew's having written the libretto for *Die schweigsame Frau* (*The Silent Woman*), Zweig recommends that the composer take on Lernet-Holenia as a librettist. In a letter dated April 12, 1935, he asks, "Are you familiar with Alexander Lernet-Holenia, one of our contemporary poets? He would seem to me just right for a work with a highly rarified style: since Hofmannsthal, the purity of his *Saul* and his *Alkestis* . . . is matched in German poetry only by Carossa. I shall be seeing him in a few days and would like to urge him to suggest a project to you. It would be a stroke of luck for you if this most noble of our dramatic talents (who also has a keen sense for the quirky and whimsical) could work with you."[4] When Richard Strauss receives the suggestion with skepticism, and a few days later even characterizes *Alkestis* as a "frightful misstep," Zweig pleads his friend's cause once more[5]: "As a writer he is a man of mystery, truly great in his poems and some dramatic scenes he has written, but then unbelievably perfunctory when writing comedies or frothy novels, which he does with one hand tied behind his back when he needs to bring in some money. Those works lack depth, but they nonetheless have a certain gracefulness. I imagine working with you on a project could stimulate him to be intensely productive, because when he catches fire, he is more terrific in my estimation than all the rest."[6] But Richard Strauss rejects the suggestion again and later settles on Joseph Gregor.

In 1936 and 1937 Lernet-Holenia writes several letters still full of empathy, but in 1938 contact between the two writers breaks off; following the *Anschluss*, the annexation of Austria by Nazi Germany, Zweig can no longer enter the country. After this event, contact with well-known Jews could create problems, and, in Sankt Wolfgang, Lernet-Holenia was under strict surveillance.

For the Zweig centenary in 1981 Hanns Arens published a letter from Lernet-Holenia that sums up his friendship with Zweig. He first recalls their collaboration on the comedy *Gelegenheit macht Liebe* (Opportunity creates love), which in his view would have had "little significance, had this play not brought the first great success to the previously unknown actress Paula Wessely."[7] Lernet-Holenia attributes Zweig's suicide to his depressive tendencies, and says not a word about the anti-Semitic attacks on Zweig or his persecution by the Nazis—any more than he commented in their correspondence on the reasons for Zweig's exile: "The strange pessimistic disintegration that brought about Zweig's end began to show itself soon after I met him, around 1926. In long conversations I tried to cheer him up. But he was so downcast that hardly anything I could say got through to him."[8]

Lernet-Holenia goes on to describe Zweig's Erasmus biography as his greatest masterpiece, and uses that work as the backdrop for interpreting Zweig's suicide as an act of heroism: "He achieved worldwide success with good, often splendid, books—but his best book, *Erasmus of Rotterdam*, hardly became known. It is a kind of autobiography. Like Erasmus—perhaps very much so—Zweig was a literary figure with a touch of the poet, a *homme de lettres* of the first order—and certainly no hero. That makes it all the more strange that he chose a hero's end."[9] He concludes, "Would that he were still here with us!"[10]

In the fall of 1957 Alexander Lernet-Holenia joined Erich Fitzbauer, Friderike Zweig, Franz Theodor Csokor, and others in founding the International Stefan Zweig Society.[11]

ARTURO LARCATI
UNIVERSITY OF VERONA

Endnotes

1. Roman Roček, *Die neun Leben des Alexander Lernet-Holenia* (Vienna: Böhlau, 1999), p. 9.

2. *"Jede Freundschaft mit mir ist verderblich": Joseph Roth und Stefan Zweig 1927–1938*, ed. Madeleine Rietra and Rainer Joachim Siegl, with an afterword by Heinz Lunzer (Göttingen: Wallstein, 2011), p. 237.

3. Donald A. Prater, *European of Yesterday: A Biography of Stefan Zweig* (Oxford: Clarendon, 1971), p. 281.

4. *Richard Strauss/Stefan Zweig, Briefwechsel*, ed. Willi Schuh (Frankfurt/Main: Fischer, 1981), p. 85.

5. Ibid., pp. 105 and 112.

6. Ibid., p. 116.

7. Lernet-Holenia, "Ich wollte, er lebte uns noch" in *Der große Europäer Stefan Zweig*, ed. and with an introduction by Hanns Arens (Frankfurt/Main: Fischer, 1981), p. 85.

8. Ibid.

9. Ibid.

10. Ibid.

11. Cf. Gert Kerschbaumer, *Stefan Zweig. Der fliegende Salzburger* (Frankfurt/Main: Fischer, 2005), p. 470.

New Directions Paperbooks—a partial listing

Kaouther Adimi, Our Riches
Adonis, Songs of Mihyar the Damascene
César Aira, Ghosts
    An Episode in the Life of a Landscape Painter
Will Alexander, Refractive Africa
Osama Alomar, The Teeth of the Comb
Guillaume Apollinaire, Selected Writings
Jessica Au, Cold Enough for Snow
Paul Auster, The Red Notebook
Ingeborg Bachmann, Malina
Honoré de Balzac, Colonel Chabert
Djuna Barnes, Nightwood
Charles Baudelaire, The Flowers of Evil*
Bei Dao, City Gate, Open Up
Mei-Mei Berssenbrugge, Empathy
Max Blecher, Adventures in Immediate Irreality
Roberto Bolaño, By Night in Chile
    Distant Star
Jorge Luis Borges, Labyrinths
    Seven Nights
Beatriz Bracher, Antonio
Coral Bracho, Firefly Under the Tongue*
Kamau Brathwaite, Ancestors
Basil Bunting, Complete Poems
Anne Carson, Glass, Irony & God
    Norma Jeane Baker of Troy
Horacio Castellanos Moya, Senselessness
Camilo José Cela, Mazurka for Two Dead Men
Louis-Ferdinand Céline
    Death on the Installment Plan
    Journey to the End of the Night
Rafael Chirbes, Cremation
Inger Christensen, alphabet
Julio Cortázar, Cronopios & Famas
Jonathan Creasy (ed.), Black Mountain Poems
Robert Creeley, If I Were Writing This
Guy Davenport, 7 Greeks
Amparo Davila, The Houseguest
Osamu Dazai, No Longer Human
    The Setting Sun
H.D., Selected Poems
Helen DeWitt, The Last Samurai
    Some Trick
Marcia Douglas
    The Marvellous Equations of the Dread
Daša Drndić, EEG
Robert Duncan, Selected Poems

Eça de Queirós, The Maias
William Empson, 7 Types of Ambiguity
Mathias Énard, Compass
Shusaku Endo, Deep River
Jenny Erpenbeck, The End of Days
    Go, Went, Gone
Lawrence Ferlinghetti
    A Coney Island of the Mind
Thalia Field, Personhood
F. Scott Fitzgerald, The Crack-Up
    On Booze
Emilio Fraia, Sevastopol
Jean Frémon, Now, Now, Louison
Rivka Galchen, Little Labors
Forrest Gander, Be With
Romain Gary, The Kites
Natalia Ginzburg, The Dry Heart
    Happiness, as Such
Henry Green, Concluding
Felisberto Hernández, Piano Stories
Hermann Hesse, Siddhartha
Takashi Hiraide, The Guest Cat
Yoel Hoffmann, Moods
Susan Howe, My Emily Dickinson
    Concordance
Bohumil Hrabal, I Served the King of England
Qurratulain Hyder, River of Fire
Sonallah Ibrahim, That Smell
Rachel Ingalls, Mrs. Caliban
Christopher Isherwood, The Berlin Stories
Fleur Jaeggy, Sweet Days of Discipline
Alfred Jarry, Ubu Roi
B.S. Johnson, House Mother Normal
James Joyce, Stephen Hero
Franz Kafka, Amerika: The Man Who Disappeared
Yasunari Kawabata, Dandelions
John Keene, Counternarratives
Heinrich von Kleist, Michael Kohlhaas
Alexander Kluge, Temple of the Scapegoat
Wolfgang Koeppen, Pigeons on the Grass
Taeko Kono, Toddler-Hunting
Laszlo Krasznahorkai, Satantango
    Seiobo There Below
Ryszard Krynicki, Magnetic Point
Eka Kurniawan, Beauty Is a Wound
Mme. de Lafayette, The Princess of Clèves
Lautréamont, Maldoror

*BILINGUAL EDITION

For a complete listing, request a free catalog from New Directions, 80 8th Avenue, New York, NY 10011 or visit us online at **ndbooks.com**